THE IRON WEDDING

JON DEL ARROZ

ISBN: 978-1-951837-06-8

ISBN (hardcover): 978-1-925645-53-8

The Iron Wedding
©2019 by Jon Del Arroz
All Rights Reserved

Cover design by Logotecture

Published in the United States of America

THE ADVENTURES OF 4 BARON VON MONOCLE

THE IRON WEDDING

JON DEL ARROZ

CHAPTER I

WHEN I *RETURNED* home from a strategy meeting with King Malaky and my father, I stumbled over a small box laid neatly in front of my apartment door.

Springtime had come in Rislandia City, a breeze blowing the cool air from the northwestern Oler Mountains. Clouds fluttered across the night sky, casting darkness over my apartment, the shadows from the buildings all around blending to obscure my vision.

Once off the main road, I didn't have the benefit of the gaslamps. Resources had been scarce since the recent Wyranth invasion, and the city's aether fuel supply had been cut to only essentials as a result.

Regardless, I should have seen the bulbous package in front of the door to my apartment. I'd been lost in thought, as I seemed to be more and more these days.

A scratching noise sounded at my front door, distracting me from the box. The scratches became more impatient as I fumbled for my keys, which I kept in a small pouch along my skirt belt. I

1

dug through coins and makeup until I caught hold of the loop at the end of the brass.

By the time I unlocked the door, a soft whimpering had joined the scratching sound.

"I'm trying. Hold your horses," I said.

I inserted the key, turned it, and opened the door.

A little rodent came scurrying out, latching itself to my skirt with its claws—my pet ferret, Toby.

The little devil had already torn half of my clothes to shreds. I was fortunate to be able to call many of those incidents "battle wear and tear", which allowed me to use the Grand Rislandian Army's tailors to stitch the fabric back together.

Even with the problems he caused my wardrobe, I still loved Toby. He'd been with me through good times and bad, the most loyal critter I could have imagined. I detached him from my skirts and brought him up into a big hug before flinging him over my shoulder as if he were a fur scarf.

He chirped in my ear.

"I missed you too," I said, crouching down to pick up the box at my feet. It was light and had a ribbon tied around it with a bow on top. A present? For me? It wasn't my birthday, and we were well past the winter festival. Curious.

I entered my apartment, considering who the gift might be from, kicking the door closed behind me. "I'm sorry, Toby, but I'm going to have to set you down."

Toby squeaked in protest but relented his grip on me. His claws pattered on my wood floor before he found his balance, and proceeded to run circles around my couch. The ritual reminded me I was low on ferret food. I'd have to remember to head to Madison's Feed Store in the morning and pick up some extra supplies. The woman kept trying to get me to take home a rabbit, but with a ferret in the house, it would have been a bad idea.

I dropped the box on a small end table and turned on the pilot to my gas lamp.

Light shone in the room, shadows falling across all of the furniture.

Even in my home, I didn't feel safe. I glanced around to make sure there weren't any invaders.

The reactive instinct wasn't paranoia. I'd had enough strange experiences where Ivan, the leader of the Wyranth Empire, had helped himself both to my apartment here and my former home in Plainsroad Village. Why he took so many risks to personally come see *me* in the heart of his enemy's territory, I couldn't say. He kept asking me to marry him on those occasions, which didn't appeal to me—to say the least.

Maybe the point was to get me jumping at shadows, panicked all of the time, where I could never rest. Making me unable to feel safe could be some strange psychological warfare tactic.

He targeted me because I commanded the world's only airship. At least, I used to, before I crashed the *Liliana* for a second time.

This time, however, I might not be getting her back again.

A sinking feeling overcame me, and I melted into my couch. Wasn't there anything I could have done to prevent the *Liliana's* destruction? The memory of my ship ramming into the strange giant creature to end the battle came flooding into my head. Debris flying everywhere. The bridge walls collapsing as the ship flipped over in the impact.

I was lucky to be alive. Even luckier that we had won the battle and saved the kingdom from certain destruction. A lot of people joked that something in my heritage predisposed me to victory, that something about being a von Monocle made me keep winning against the odds.

It didn't feel like much of a win. A sense of isolation loomed over me. Useless without my ship and her crew.

The feeling had been with me for months. It didn't seem right for me to have some fancy apartment in the city, paid for by the kingdom, while I did little to pull my weight. I sat in meetings with generals, where I had no right to be as a seventeen-year-old girl. I should be happy with everything I'd received in this life, but I found it harder and harder to be content.

I needed a purpose.

My elbow bumped the box on my end table. I'd nearly forgotten about it.

I picked it up again, this time viewing it in the soft light my lamp offered. The box was white, and the bowed ribbon was a deep crimson.

I reached for the ends of the ribbon, but my thoughts got the best of me again. What if this was trap? Some ploy to blow up in my face?

All kinds of dangerous scenarios ran through my head. I couldn't put anything past the Wyranth.

Or could I?

Ivan had never tried to harm me in our encounters. He'd always treated me cordially, even allowed me to point a gun at him while he assured me I was safe.

Would he send a package to me as a trick?

I didn't even know if it was from him.

Deep breath. Calm down. The gift probably came from one of my friends, or maybe even my father. I shouldn't panic at a box. Besides, it was far too light to have anything like an explosive inside. Or so I hoped.

I pulled on the ribbon. It came apart easily, the fabric gliding as I unwrapped it from around the box. I lifted the box top.

A note rested inside, and on it, another piece of deep crimson fabric, but this fabric appeared to be one piece and took up the whole interior of the box. The note read:

Zaira,

I realized during my last mission I never had the opportunity to get you a birthday present. I wasn't sure what I should get for you, so I hope you like it. I also hope you'll wear it to dinner with me tomorrow night. Meet me at the Knights' barracks. I'll have another surprise.

Love,

Ethan von Lantern

Ethan! Of course, he'd be the one to give me a gift. What was I thinking? Silly girl. I shook my head and laughed at myself. He and I had been getting closer since The Battle of Rislandia City, as it was now being called. We'd exchanged a couple of kisses, but timing and duty got in the way of any formal relationship.

It always would. He would be off as a knight somewhere, risking his life, and I would be off...

I didn't want to think about the airship again. I should focus on Ethan. He had been thoughtful enough to get me a gift. How sweet of him.

My heart fluttered at the thought of his strong chin and kind smile, his brown eyes shining at me. He was both so tender and so strong at the same time. Everything I could ever dream of in a man. I really should have made more time for him over the months I'd known him. Who knew when either of us would draw our last breaths?

Toby crawled onto the couch and pressed himself against my thigh, sensing my depressing thoughts.

"I'm sorry, Toby," I said, stroking his furry head. "I need to get better about thinking positively. I have to find something to do."

This dinner date Ethan proposed might be the ticket. I could go out with him, enjoy a night out on the town, and live like a normal person. Even if it were for just one night.

I scooped the fabric into my hand, lifting an elegant red dress. The material had a soft, silky quality to it, and it had a golden trim. The colors of Rislandia. It made me smile. Ethan always thought so patriotically, even in the littlest of gestures. It further endeared him to me, as I loved this kingdom as much as he did.

I stood, holding the dress to my body. It pressed against my chest and draped down to my ankles. Ethan had figured out my measurements. Should I make something of that? Boys only had one-track minds.

Upon further inspection of the dress, it was appropriate for a formal gown, something I could wear to any occasion in the city and look regal. I'd never owned a dress like this, despite coming to the city several months prior. When I'd been a farm girl back in Plainsroad Village, I would have died to try on a dress like this. Ethan had probably spent a small fortune on it.

I had to admit, I was impressed. No one had ever gone to this length for me before. Tears formed in my eyes, and I bit down on my lip to stop them. No. I wouldn't cry about this. What was wrong with me?

I had to calm down and get a good night's sleep. "Let's turn in a little early, Toby. No reading tonight. We have a big day tomorrow. I need to get you some more food, and I'm going to have the night of my life."

Toby sniffed the area around the couch, ignoring my proclamation.

I laid the dress neatly back into the box, not wanting to wrinkle it, or risk Toby getting his paws on it. Then, I sealed the box and readied myself for bed. Hopefully tonight, unlike most nights, sleep would come.

CHAPTER 2

THE NEXT DAY dragged on forever.

All I wanted to do was to rush into the evening and meet Ethan. I had so many mundane tasks to do first to keep my apartment in order—including making sure I got food for Toby. Plus, my father hit me with the worst of all possible jobs—he had a stack of paperwork in his office he needed filed. Since I was out of a real job in the war effort for the foreseeable future, he drafted me for it.

"Thank you!" My father said before I could open my mouth to protest.

He bounded out the door, leaving me stuck with the work.

Nothing made the time go by faster. Every time I looked at the clock on the wall in the back office of the Grand Rislandian Army's headquarters, ticking ahead, its gears turning, the time had hardly changed at all.

After a while, the rhythm of the clock's ticking drove me mad. But I wanted to finish the task so I wouldn't have to come back the next day and do the same thing.

The hours whittled by with me plopping papers into various rows in wooden filing cabinets with brass tracks. Service records, pay stubs—the pile had so many items. It was amazing my father had let them pile up this much. But who else had the time to stop and organize anything in recent months?

When I finished, the sun had begun to set. I had to clean up and get ready.

I rushed back to my apartment, flipping the switch to my gas water heater, waiting for the tub to fill with water. I wouldn't have much time to take a proper bath, and I didn't want to be late for Ethan. He would be expecting me in minutes.

I jumped in, the water scalding, but I couldn't wait for it to cool to the right temperature. I cleaned myself quickly, and got out without draining the tub. It would have to wait until later.

I dried my body, and then used a new hand-crank hair drier, which shot warm air onto my hair, removing the moisture and giving it more fluff. I slipped into my undergarments and then went to work on my makeup and hair in front of the mirror.

These parts of my readying routine couldn't be rushed. I had to look my best. I wanted just enough blush on my cheeks, some good definition to my skin, and for my eyelashes to appear much thicker than they naturally were—but not clumpy. The process of applying my face typically relaxed me, but knowing I was on a tight deadline, it brought me more stress.

Finally, I slipped into the dress. It hugged me around the hips a little more than I thought proper. With the meticulous care Ethan put into the gift, I had to believe that was intentional. Boys, I swear.

The cumulative effect of my rosy cheeks and dirty blonde hair flowing down to my back over the crimson was wonderful. I looked *fantastic*. I spun around, letting the bottom of the dress flow as if I were at a formal ball. The dress looked even better on me than it had out of the box.

Toby squawked at me, bringing me out of the trance of my routine.

"I'm sorry, I have to go!" I told him.

I deftly avoided my ferret's attempts to cuddle with me—and his attempts to cling to my brand-new dress—stepping around him and into the main room of my apartment to find something to slip on my feet. I didn't have the best shoes for this attire. All I had was a leather shoe that tied in the front. It at least gave me a little bit of a heel and opening on the top of my foot. Better than combat boots.

The dress covered most of the shoes, thankfully, and I hurried out the door before Toby could command my attention again.

Jogging wasn't easy in these shoes, so I moved at a brisk walk down the steps of my apartment and across the path toward the courtyard where the knights had their barracks.

Standing at the end of the courtyard, overlooking the knights' facilities, the palace, and the rest of the city, a giant stone lookout shot to the sky. The view of the Crystal Spire took my breath away no matter how many times I saw it. Lights beamed from the top of it, a constant reminder of what ancient Rislandians had built here, and the level of achievement we had to defend. Renewed pride for my kingdom and this city filled me, giving me warmth.

The touch of a strong hand fell on my shoulder, causing me to jump. I stifled my breath and turned.

Ethan von Lantern stood in front of me, wearing a dashing pinstripe brown suit with a vest beneath his coat. I'd never seen him wear this before, as he typically wore his leathers that identified the knights. It looked a little tight around the shoulders and arms, the suit unable to fully contain his muscular form.

I didn't get to see much of his brown eyes, because they closed as he leaned in for a kiss.

I melted into him, letting him hold me against him with the slip of his arm behind my back. I closed my eyes, and let myself go, drowning in his warmth.

His lips touched mine, with confidence equal to how he'd grabbed my shoulder. He knew what he wanted. He was here for me. I couldn't imagine anything more glorious—until my lips parted.

The heat of the moment was like someone struck a match and lit my whole body on fire. I didn't know if it was possible to lose myself more in Ethan's kiss, but he could work miracles. Recalling we were in a public place, I pulled back, forcing myself to breathe.

"That's one way to greet a girl," I said.

Ethan chuckled. "My favorite way." His eyes scanned my whole body, and as they did, they seemed to grow wider. "My gift went well."

"Oh, Ethan! This is the most amazing thing anyone's ever given me. Thank you."

The words brought a smile to his face. "I'm glad," he said. "Now for part two of the gift. Come with me."

Ethan took me by the hand and walked me toward the Crystal Spire. I wondered what he had in store, but followed without a word, happy to have my hand in his, our fingers interlocking.

We entered the base of the spire, and Ethan made his way to the spiral steps. Part of me wanted to protest that he should have warned me we were going to walk to the top of the giant structure. These shoes were not designed for a long hike. Neither was the dress I wore. The walk to the top of the spire made my feet sore and my body uncomfortable.

At least Ethan slowed his pace and allowed us a leisurely walk. He understood I wasn't nearly in the shape he was.

We passed the lower levels where landings branched off to the High Knight's office and then continued up the spire's hundreds of steps. I tugged on Ethan's hand about halfway up and made him let me take a break. We looked out through the window to a beautiful view of Rislandia City. Even though there were minimal lights on, the city looked elegant from this level.

"Almost as beautiful as you," Ethan said.

I prodded him in the side. "Now you're being silly."

Ethan laughed. "I'm not. I promise!"

We continued up the stairs.

Eventually, we reached the top. Ethan helped me out onto the landing, where a cool breeze blew across us. I shivered. Ethan noticed this, removing his coat and placing it around my shoulders.

"Thanks," I said, drawing his coat tightly around me. It had a musky scent, just like Ethan. It was nice to have it close.

A table rested on the landing, set with a cloth, with several candles on it. Two other knights I vaguely recognized hovered around the table, making sure the settings were in place. A small tray rested to the side holding a platter, covered with a silver top.

"Your dinner awaits," Ethan said, motioning to the table.

I wanted to cry again.

All of this? For me? I couldn't believe his extreme efforts. I would have been happy just scrounging a meal. This was incredible. How many people in the world were able to have dinner with such a beautiful view? I was thankful the night was much clearer than the one prior, because I could see the silhouettes of the landscapes beyond Rislandia city from the light of the stars and moon. It was perfect.

But I had to keep myself composed. Ethan couldn't keep his eyes off of me, and I didn't want him to think something was wrong when I cried from joy.

He held my chair for me, and slid it inward as I sat, then moved around to his own side of the table to take his seat. "Glass of wine? I had Reggie grab a bottle of an old reserve."

I shook my head. "I'm not into drinking, sorry." Truth was, I hadn't tried wine before. I still felt a little too young for it, and I'd seen drunken men. It scared me, even though I realized we weren't likely to push drinking that far. Ethan was enough of an intoxicant for me.

The other two knights hovered about us. One poured water for me, while still pouring Ethan a glass of wine. The other removed the cover from the platter and revealed two plates, which he picked up and set before us.

The sight of juicy steak, with some vegetable garnish made my mouth water. It must have been difficult to secure the meat, with the Wyranth having razed so much of our farmland. Our soldiers' rations comprised of small cakes of grain and bacon, foods much easier to produce and store than the meal before me. Ethan had outdone himself again. I hadn't had a meal like this since I'd had the pleasure of the *Liliana's* chef to cook for me. My mouth watered looking at it.

Ethan picked up his fork and knife, motioning to me. "Go ahead," he said.

I did my best to be a good, dainty woman. I didn't usually take such care with the way I handled silverware, but this was an occasion. The meat invited the fork and knife, tender, and cutting easily. Juices dripped from it onto my plate, and I took my first bite. The taste was so savory, it alone made the evening worth it.

"This is amazing," I said.

"I'm glad you like it," Ethan said. "It's funny, when I first tried to prepare the meal, I thought of seafood. I'm better at preparing fish, but I wasn't sure if you'd like it."

"We didn't get much fish in Plainsroad Village," I said.

"I figured that. I asked James for your preferences," Ethan said, and then grimaced. "It cost me, too."

"I probably don't want to know."

"You're probably right."

His dark eyes met mine, and locked there. I forgot to breathe again, let alone eat. I wanted him to jump over the table and kiss me again, even with the other knights standing there. But I could be patient. I forced myself to chew another bite. "You're from Shellville, right?" I asked after swallowing the piece of meat.

"Born and raised. I haven't had time to go back there yet since the invasion," he said.

"Oh, no," I said. My heart went out to him. I knew how hard it was to lose a home.

Shellville was just south of Portsgate, and we'd seen the devastation the Wyranth had caused in our larger coastal city.

JON DEL ARROZ

They didn't even wait around and hold the area, but razed the whole city on their multi-pronged march toward Rislandia City. I wasn't sure what I should ask about the topic. It could be a sensitive one, and I didn't want to ruin the mood.

"I did get word my family's alive. They took to their boats when the Wyranth came, fled to Sun's Rest. The Wyranth went on to Portsgate. I've got a letter saying there was a lot of damage, but I'm not sure the extent of it," he said.

At least he still had his family. Unlike James. Poor James! I understood well the feeling of losing family. It was like a hole in one's life one could never get back. Except, in my case, I did. My father wasn't really dead. "Smart of them," I said.

"Yeah, I guess I come from good stock like that."

I snorted. "Arrogant much?"

Ethan grinned. "Just honest about my capabilities."

He made me laugh. That was a large part of why I liked him. Anything to make me forget the realities of being grounded, useless after having a taste of the adventuring my father used to write home about.

"Something the matter?" Ethan asked. He was too observant.

"I'm okay," I said, dabbing my mouth with a napkin.

"You're touching your face. You do that when you're nervous or not being honest," he said. It wasn't judgmental the way he said it, just matter of fact.

"How do you—?"

"I've had a lot of practice watching people," he said.

I nodded. "Yeah. You're right. I hate waiting here in the city. I want to be back out there." I motioned my fork to the land beyond, the vast expanse of dark shadows in the night. Who knew what was out there?

"It'll happen eventually," Ethan said.

"Not if Harkerpal can't find a way to get the airship back up and running. He's gone crazy trying. There's something missing, and we still don't know what."

13

"He'll find it. Have faith. For now," Ethan said, "enjoy the rest of your time here. Who knows how much longer we'll have to be together like this?"

I smiled at him. He cared about me. My cheeks radiated heat despite the night air. "You're right. I wish I could stop thinking."

Ethan met my eyes. "Don't we all."

For a while, I enjoyed the moment with him. We spent the rest of the evening together. Everything he'd planned for me was glorious, from the chocolate dessert, to the way we stood at the edge of the top of the spire and looked out upon the city, talking. It was beautiful.

He was beautiful.

But it wouldn't last forever.

CHAPTER 3

A MESSENGER ARRIVED at my home in the early morning to tell me a horseless carriage was waiting for me. My father and a team were surveying the progress on the rebuilt airship, which was being reconstructed where we'd crashed north of Rislandia City.

I yawned, tired from staying out far too late with Ethan. We had enough presence of mind between us to call our evening quits before the sun came up, but it couldn't have been much before dawn when he walked me back to my apartment and retired to his quarters.

This day would be a long one.

I readied myself and followed the messenger to the street where the carriage waited, a black hunk of metal with big tires and a huge steamstack protruding from the center of it. The motor *whirred* and exhaust trickled into the air.

My father and his bride, Talyen, sat in the carriage. Talyen had already lost the baby weight she'd gained from carrying Lilly, and was back into fighting shape with her form well-defined in her Grand Rislandian Army grey uniform, complete with cap. On her right breast was a brass pendant of the Crest of Malaky, the gear with angel wings and a crown atop it. On her left was the Rislandian Medal of Valor.

My father also wore a uniform, which looked strange on him. Despite being such an integral part of the army, he used to dress as I now did, in a white shirt with a red cape. He'd passed the look onto me, though he used to wear a top hat along with the ensemble. I'd abandoned the hat ever since the airship crashed. It flattened my hair when I wore it.

The clean, military appearance made my father look older than before, but also more distinguished. He had a freshly trimmed salt and pepper beard, and wrinkles lined his face, but his bright eyes betrayed a youthful spirit.

"Zaira," my father called. "I'm glad you can make it. Hop in the back with Talyen."

"I hope you've been well," Talyen said.

"As well as can be. Who's got Lilly?" I asked.

"Our nanny. You really should come by more to play with your sister," Talyen said.

I'd neglected Lilly, as I had many of my other relationships. I hadn't been in the mood to spend time with anyone as of late, Ethan's company excepted. But Ethan had been the one to make the effort in our relationship. I found people to be taxing. I didn't mean that in an arrogant way, but more because I couldn't get comfortable around anyone else. What use could I be to anyone without my airship? Maybe today, Harkerpal and his engineers would have some better news.

I made my way around the side of the car to the vacant seat and helped myself to it. The messenger drove, and soon the carriage putted down the cobblestone streets of the city, through the gates, and out to the open road of the hilled countryside surrounding Rislandia City.

The road followed a river for a way, and then split off to the north. It was a beautiful spring day, and though the speed of the horseless carriage caused wind to blow in our faces, it was a nice ride. Not too hot, not too cold.

After about an hour's ride, we reached the airship reconstruction site, the place where the *Liliana* had originally crashed. I hadn't been here since the frame construction, but I'd sat in several of the meetings where Harkerpal warned he didn't think he would be able to make her fly again.

Those meetings sapped the energy from me.

My heart lifted, though, at the breathtaking view of the new ship. She had new side paneling, much more ornate than before, with the Crest of Malaky carved into the side planks, and a nice trim at the front with swirls and frills. They turned the new *Liliana* into a work of art worthy of what she'd been before.

In addition to the turbines up top, it now had two propellers dangling on either side of the ship, large blades as large as my apartment, resting just front of center and facing forward, attached like small wings to the side of the craft at the rear.

Cranes hovered over the ship. They looked much like our horseless carriage, but with big metal arms attached to them, along with gears and mechanical cranks to lift the arms up and down, though they weren't in use now.

We pulled up to a series of tents set in front of the ship, where dozens of army engineers worked. Harkerpal stood, his dark skin and lanky figure immediately recognizable. He hunched over a table with large paper plans, pointing and directing his men.

We got out of the carriage as a group, following my father as he led the way toward Harkerpal and his engineering crew. My father shielded his eyes from the sun to get a better look at the *Liliana*. "You know, I think the new design looks nice, but I can't help but long for the old, simpler version. I must have spent too many years on the ship."

"I like the new look," I said.

He glanced back at me, giving an expression like he wanted to argue, but then he grinned. "That's what's important. She's yours now."

If the *Liliana* ever graced the skies again.

We didn't say any more before reaching Harkerpal.

"I remember the first time I rebuilt the engine," the engineer said to his men. "We took it completely apart, taking brushes with fine metal wire on the end and a polishing concoction made by an alchemic specialist, Dr. Busse. Made quite interesting potions, though I lost track of her after the first Wyranth invasion. We— "

"Harkerpal!" My father called to him.

Harkerpal bobbed his head in the reflexive way he often did, his eyes brightening. "Theodore! I mean... General."

"No need for formalities," my father said, a little bounce in his step as he moved to Harkerpal. He greeted the engineer with a hug. "What's the good word? Have you figured out how to make her fly yet?"

Harkerpal acknowledged both Talyen and me before returning his attention to my father. "That's what I'm trying to go over with my team. We're trying to recall back as far as we can. I'm quite sure we've brought the engine back to the specifications I have, but there's something missing."

"Have you fired her up today?" my father asked.

"No."

"Perhaps all it needs is some von Monocle luck?" My father beamed.

"It's worth a try."

Harkerpal waved for a couple of his men to follow him, and we all ventured toward the airship. The ramp lowered, allowing us entry in to the bottom cargo bay, which led to a path to the engine room.

Overall, the room looked like I remembered it, but a little cleaner. No oil or soot dirtied the big engine area. The furnace stood erect in the back, with the gears and pistons that turned the great turbines nested above. One of Harkerpal's men grabbed a canister full of aether fuel, pouring some into a small hatch that flowed down a transparent tube into the tank. The fuel both lubricated the engine and provided the necessary energy to fire the motor.

"I miss the smell of aether fuel," my father said.

"Too much of it can cause problems," Harkerpal said. "Do you remember the time we were on a diplomatic mission to Panderica, and Ensign Carson thought the crew had turned into vampiric pookas?"

My father chuckled. "It took four of us to hold him down before the medic could sedate him."

"Ahh, the good old days," Harkerpal said. He moved and turned a crank which started the engine.

It roared, and then whirred as the gears turned, smoothing its sound into a soft rumble.

Harkerpal closed his eyes. "Sounds just like I remember her."

"That's good," my father said.

The engineer opened his eyes again. "But, despite the engine working, and the turbines moving, we can't quite get them up to speeds as before. Even with the addition of the wing propellers we don't have enough force to lift the wooden hull off the ground. It's simple physics, the weight of the *Liliana* is just too much to fly, even with the new, lighter design upgrades."

"But we flew before," my father said.

"That's what I don't understand," Harkerpal said, frowning at the engine mechanism.

"Can we redesign the ship to weigh less?" I asked.

"It'd have to be a complete overhaul, starting from scratch," Harkerpal said. "We're working on different flying mechanisms. We're very close to completing work on single-man fliers based on my observations of the bat gliders we saw on Zenwey."

Those bat gliders gave us quite a scare. The Nightmen used them and circled around our ship. If it weren't for some timely natural help from a volcano, we might not have come back from the strange continent. "That sounds promising," I said. It also wasn't an airship. I wouldn't be able to command it. All I wanted was for the *Liliana* to work.

"There has to be something we overlooked," Harkerpal said. "I've been pouring over the plans, but I can't figure out what it is.

There must be one more component that's missing. If only Dr. du Brass was still with us."

"Who's that?" I asked.

"The original designer of the airship," my father said. "He was a brilliant man whose imagination and innovation has never been matched. No offense, Harkerpal."

"None taken," Harkerpal said. "I could never hope to replace him."

The room fell silent save for the sound of the engine.

I wished we still had the plans to the ship I'd found in Plainsroad Village. They were in the airship when we crashed, and no one had been able to find them afterward. We had been so close with those, and now we needed them more than ever.

It might have been better if I'd left the plans buried in a hidden compartment in my former home, but I couldn't have known that at the time. Besides, the Wyranth kept us on our toes, their soldiers stalking us. If we'd left the plans, they might have fallen into their hands. If the Wyranth managed to create an airship, our lives would be far worse.

My father crossed his arms. "If we can't get her flying, we'll have to divert our resources elsewhere. There's too much manpower being spent on this ship we could be using in more fruitful efforts."

"I concur," Harkerpal said, sadness in his voice.

He loved the ship as much as any of us did. He'd spent countless hours in this engine room over the years. The *Liliana* was a part of him. I couldn't imagine how it felt for him to lose her.

My father sighed. "Two more days. If you can't come up with something, we shut the project down."

I wanted to argue. We all did. But there was nothing to say. My father was right. We would have to move on. But how could I be Baron von Monocle without an airship? What would I do with my life?

The prospect made my chest constrict. Thinking about it horrified me. And for everyone here, it would be the most demoralizing blow possible. The airship was more than just a weapon, it was a symbol of hope for Rislandia.

If Harkerpal couldn't get her to fly, our country would never be the same.

CHAPTER 4

WE RETURNED TO Rislandia City in the late afternoon, after my father discussed more plans with the engineers and met with the troops stationed there. It wasn't a bad day overall, but I still had to linger around and watch without adding much to any of the conversations. I was tired of sitting and waiting. I wanted to *do* something.

The war effort was going well. We kept advancing southward on our positions, and the Wyranth hadn't recovered from the blows we'd dealt to them. We might be able to return the kingdom to its normal border soon.

The only issue came from a lack of resources.

Because the Wyranth had gone scorched earth in their advance upon our nation, we didn't have the influx of goods from the southern cities and towns, or those on the western coast, like we typically had by this time of year. Some towns—like my former home of Plainsroad Village—had been abandoned, while others were busy with full reconstruction efforts. We tried to sequester as many supplies as possible for the military, but we were hardly up to full strength.

My airship still proved to be a substantive drain on what we had.

The next step wouldn't be abandoning the ship, but I knew if we couldn't find a way to get her airborne soon, we would have to repurpose the parts for other machinery. I dreaded having that talk with my father.

But perhaps we could find some way of making the airship work.

As I departed the horseless carriage and said my goodbyes, my mind reeled trying to come up with any possible solution.

I entered the courtyard where the knights trained. Ethan or James might have an idea. They were resourceful.

Several knights sparred with swords in one room, but my friends weren't among them. Others walked and talked. It wasn't mealtime yet, so they wouldn't be in their mess.

Giving up finding them on my own, I stopped one of the knights who stood beneath an awning. He pointed me to the offices, not in the Crystal Spire where the top ranked knights worked, but spaces for general use close to the palace. The structures surrounding the courtyard were so vast I hardly knew what was where. I much preferred navigating around the few cramped rooms of an airship.

Eventually, I found my friends. James had his feet up on a desk, lounging and leaning his chair backward on two legs. He didn't see me as I entered, deep in conversation with Ethan.

I grabbed the back of his chair and tugged it toward me to give him a scare.

James flailed his arms, gasping as he lost his balance, though he quickly recovered.

He looked up at me, dark brown eyes still holding fear from my stunt, his brown bangs falling into his face. James pushed his bangs aside. "By Malaky, Zair-bear, you scared me half to death."

"You shouldn't lean back on your chair," I said, pushing it forward so the other two legs clanked on the ground. "And you need a haircut."

"Okay, *Mom*," James said, mocking me.

I wanted to tell him he could use a motherly figure, but much as I'd lost my own, James had been orphaned. It would have been a knife twist even for me to rib him with the comment. "Doesn't Princess Reina look out for you these days? I'm surprised she lets her beau exist in such an unkempt state."

"Hey," James said. His eyes narrowed in a devilish manner.

I smiled sweetly to him.

"Okay, you two," Ethan said. "No fighting in my office. I don't want to see James get his butt kicked by a girl."

"Double hey!" James said, glaring at Ethan.

We all broke out laughing. It was nice to joke around again. I'd missed having fun with the two of them. It seemed like ages ago we'd set out on my airship, wide-eyed and innocent, on an adventure across the sea to the Zenwey Continent. We were just kids then. We should have been kids now, but circumstances dictated our swift maturation. I sighed.

"What're you two plotting?" I asked.

Ethan got up from his seat and circled the desk to give me a hug. "We're talking about our next mission."

"Oh?" I said after the embrace, drawing back from him.

"Yeah. We're gonna go to Nyanzi," James said.

"That's pretty far from here, isn't it?" I asked.

Ethan nodded. "It is. I was going to come find you shortly to break the news to you. We might be gone for a good while. Without airship travel, we're going to have to travel by sea."

"What's out in Nyanzi? I don't think I've heard much about that country," I said.

"Neither have I," James said. "We found a letter from a machinist to a Wyranth scientist. They're developing mechanized units to fight against us," James said. "We're going to try to find their facility and take it out."

"Or see if we can appropriate the machinery," Ethan said.

I leaned against the back wall. "Sounds fun."

"This is the kind of assignment I've been waiting for." James rubbed his hands together.

His eyes twinkled in hunger, but then he usually had intense eagerness when he had a chance at action.

I envied them. I wished I could go on a mission to a foreign land, but I would just slow them down. James and Ethan had become quite the team in the last several months. There were whispers about them all through the upper circles of the military, all positive. I wouldn't tell them that, however. They didn't need bigger heads.

Ethan reached for my hand, took it, and gave me a soft squeeze. "It looks like our evening the other night will be our last together."

"You're leaving that soon?"

"Yeah," Ethan said.

I bit my lip. What would I do without Ethan here? My days would become even more mundane and miserable. The world conspired against my happiness. "I was hoping to talk to both of you about something else," I said. I laid out the day's events, and the issues with the airship.

Ethan nodded and listened along attentively, while James drifted off into his own thoughts. I wanted to box his ears, but restrained myself.

Once I finished my story, Ethan wrinkled his forehead, considering. "Now that you mention it, I'd wondered how the airship took flight. Being unable to take off because of weight makes a lot of sense."

I crossed my arms. "You're not being useful."

"Sorry," Ethan said. "James?"

James stroked his chin. "Search me. Give me a sword and point me at a target. I'm no engineer."

"Useless," I said.

"Sorry," Ethan said. "I wish we had better answers."

"If Harkerpal can't figure it out, I doubt anyone can," James said.

What had I been hoping for? Of course, this would be their answer. I had been foolish in thinking they'd tell me anything different. I didn't want to believe this was the end of the airship and my career as an adventurer. The reality of the situation set in like walls closing in on me. I pulled my arms in a little more tightly around myself.

Ethan motioned his head at James. "Mind giving us a second?"

James pushed back on his chair and stood. "Sure." As he passed by me, he gave me a pat on the shoulder. "Cheer up, Zair-bear. Ethan won't be gone forever. A few weeks, tops."

"Thanks," I said.

When he had left the room, Ethan moved closer to me. He pried my arms apart, his fingertips sliding down my wrists until he found my hands, linking his with mine. "I'm sorry, Zaira. If I could make the airship fly for you, I would."

"I know," I said, casting my eyes aside. My cheeks grew hot.

"This is probably the worst time to leave. We finally have something good going. I wish I could be in two places at once."

"Your duty's most important," I said, meeting his eyes again.

His lips tensed, his expression sad and brooding, but still he remained much stronger than me.

Ethan brought me a sense of comfort and safety, even without my airship giving me the sense of home. In some other world, we might have gone back to his fishing village on the coast and had a family. But that wasn't the life for either of us. He couldn't stop working for the kingdom any more than I could.

"It is. I serve the king first," Ethan said, as if realizing. He had a sheepish expression.

"It's okay. It's what I love about you," I said.

My mouth became dry. I'd never used that word with him before.

Love.

I loved him.

His eyes brightened at the word. "I love you too," he said.

"We'll end this war, and I'll find a way to get the airship flying again. Then, you and I can travel the world, exploring and making epic tales just like my father used to do," I said.

Ethan paused for a moment, staring at me, as if trying to see through to my soul. "Yes, I think we will."

Before I could say another word, he leaned in and kissed me. His body pressed against mine, pinning me to the wall. I opened myself to him. I wanted to be with him forever.

The kiss raged with fiery heat, more impassioned than any from the prior night. Both Ethan and I knew this might be our last. All of the flames of our desire for each other had to burn strong here. It was a kiss to remember.

He finally broke the kiss, but didn't pull back from me. My breath quickened, my heart beating harder than I could ever remember.

"Thank you," he said.

I chuckled. "For letting you kiss me?"

"For understanding me," Ethan said.

A shiver went down my spine. I understood exactly what he meant. "Thank you for understanding me, too," I said, words barely able to escape my lips. "Come back safe, okay?"

Ethan nodded, and then he kissed me one more time.

CHAPTER 5

I RECEIVED A surprise visit from one of the king's personal servants.

"Ms. von Monocle, your presence is requested in the main audience chamber," he said.

"Am I going to have to dress the part?" I asked, recalling the first time I'd come to Rislandia City and had to wear the poofy monstrosities required of citizens gaining audience with the king. He hadn't made me wear them in a while, but it still amused me to ask.

"Why, no, Ms. von Monocle," the servant stuttered. "You're allowed—"

"I'm messing with you. Show me the way," I said.

The servant led me into the palace and through the big doors with unmoving, statue-like guards. I wasn't sure they even blinked.

People cluttered the chamber. King Malaky sat on his throne on a raised dais. Mr. du Gearsmith stood beside him on one side, with my father on the other. Princess Reina sat daintily on a seat to the right of the king, hands folded in her lap, wearing an elegant green dress that emphasized her finer feminine qualities. I envied her appearance, though she smiled fondly at me in acknowledgement.

Two more soldiers stood guard inside, surrounding a group of people I didn't recognize. At the center of the entourage stood a tall man, pale skinned with a dark beard that came to a point on his chin. He fidgeted with something in his hand that appeared as if it were a small rock. His eyes bored into me like an electrical charge. They were deep blues that reminded me of...

The Iron Emperor. I gasped.

Those were his eyes, but this certainly wasn't him. Could it be some relation of his? This group had to be Wyranth.

The servant led me closer to the group, who engaged in small talk, stopping as I was recognized. The servant cleared his throat. "Announcing the Baron Zaira von Monocle, captain of the airship *Liliana*."

The title stung. I was the *former* captain of the airship. Everyone in this room knew it. I approached the throne, curtsying and bowing low.

"Zaira," King Malaky said, inclining his head to me. Irritation twisted in his voice. "You're just in time."

The delegation of Wyranth turned to me.

"Ah, Ms. von Monocle," Mr. Du Gearsmith said. "I should introduce you to our guest. Please meet Andrei Zelezo, ambassador from the Wyranth Empire, here all the way from the Wyranth capital."

I hadn't noticed it when I'd entered, ready for a fairly uneventful meeting with the king, but everyone in the room watched with trepidation. Eyes were alert, especially the Rislandians, and the king held tight in his posture. He looked a little paler than usual, which I'd first attributed to the sickness plaguing him, but it could have come from the stress of the Wyranth in these chambers.

The king had more to his sickly look than just being pale. His skin glistened with some sweat, his hair looking thinner than usual, and grayer than I remembered. This war had taken its toll on all of us.

I swallowed. Why did I have an awful sinking feeling?

"It's good she's here," Andrei said. His voice sounded just as much like Ivan's as his eyes carried the penetrating blue colors. Deep, captivating. The Iron Emperor would have been a charming man if he hadn't been so creepy. This man proved very similar, even in his mannerisms. But this body and face didn't match. "I'd been looking forward to meeting you." He grinned at me.

"Are you related to Ivan?" I asked. I realized after it came out I'd used the Iron Emperor's name—which almost no one knew.

Andrei appeared startled. "We all are related to the father of our country," he said, turning back to face King Malaky. "Thank you, generous king, for allowing me an audience within your chamber. I know our people have been at odds as of late..."

"Your people have killed thousands of Rislandians," King Malaky said.

Andrei tugged at the collar of his shirt. "War is an ugly thing. But I am here to parley, not to continue the fighting. Please, I understand your feelings in regard to my people, but can we have a productive talk?" He placed his hand on his chest.

King Malaky looked as if he wanted to spit at the Wyranth. "I'm listening," he said. "Make it quick."

Andrei pulled a small piece of paper from his pocket, which he proceeded to unfold. "I am here on authority of the Iron Emperor to discuss an armistice between our peoples. The war has been a long and bloody one, and it is time for our countries to return to a peaceful coexistence which benefits the both of us. Our proposal would be for the Wyranth Empire to extend northward to Lake Bethany, with the new border stretching to the southern end of the Twin lakes. The Rislandians agree to cede Pleasant Pass, Desert's Watch, Lakeside, Borderville, Swantown, Twin Tops Village, Murkfort, and the Southern Vale to the Wyranth Empire. In exchange, the Wyranth are willing to pull our troops from all holdings to the west of the Westerly Spine, and retreat from Loveridge and Centerpost to allow Rislandia to reclaim those settlements."

"Preposterous," Mr. du Gearsmith said.

King Malaky reclined into his throne. The mere act of sitting upright appeared to tax him. "I'm inclined to agree with my advisor. Our military is steadily gaining on the holdings you're proposing on retreating from. We would be giving up nearly the entire southern region of our country, and for what?"

Andrei blinked as though it were obvious. "To stop the bloodshed. Isn't a little land worth it?"

"Why not give up all the land you stole?" King Malaky asked.

Andrei shook his head, folding the paper in half and then in quarters before stuffing it in his pocket. "I'm afraid that would be impossible. The empire needs the land. The purpose here is to compromise. The area around the Border River has been in dispute since we were children, and for generations before that if you take into account historical conflicts. It's not something we have to decide upon today, but the offer is open." He snapped his fingers together. "However, there is a smaller matter I wish to discuss before retiring. If we can open dialogue on one front, we might be able to work toward a future where the fighting can stop in earnest?"

Princess Reina rolled her eyes. I wanted to punch the man. He had such a smarmy attitude to him, as if we were his playthings. Where did he get off treating us like this?

"I'm listening," King Malaky said quickly. Whether it was because he was irritated with the Wyranth or because he found sitting in the chamber to be taxing in his condition, I couldn't tell.

"I understand your airship's been grounded," Andrei said.

The words sent a jolt down my spine. I tensed my shoulders and my eyes widened.

"That's right," King Malaky said.

"Our informants have let us know your reconstruction's nearly complete, but there's a missing element to the engine. The airship is too heavy to lift off and it needs an extra jolt of power the current engine can't provide. Does that sound accurate?" Andrei asked, a grin plastered on his face.

"Don't give him more information than we have to, your majesty," Mr. du Gearsmith said.

Andrei waved off the lanky advisor. "Please. I'm being forthright with you. We have full information as to the workings of your airship. It's a top priority for our intelligence."

King Malaky nodded, turning his head to Mr. du Gearsmith, his eyes shifting. "Not to worry, counterintelligence is well aware of the situation."

I raised a brow. Was King Malaky bluffing?

"I assure you, there's no need to posture," Andrei said. "You see, we have the means for you to repair your airship, and we are willing to give them to you so you can get her flying again." He made a motion with his hand as if it were the *Liliana* floating through the air.

"And what would you want for that? Rislandia City?" Princess Reina chimed in, snorting.

"Nothing so preposterous," Andrei said.

"Then what?" King Malaky asked.

Andrei turned to me. "The Iron Emperor requests Ms. Zaira von Monocle's hand in marriage in exchange for our airship plans."

The room fell silent. I couldn't help but burst out laughing.

"You can't be serious," I said.

"Deadly so," Andrei said.

My laughter stopped. All eyes shifted to me. I wanted to shrink away. How could I be put on the spot like this in front of everyone? It was embarrassing. I could hardly believe it was real. This had to be a ploy to throw us off guard—something.

"This is quite the matter to deliberate upon," King Malaky said. "I'm not going to force my subject to do anything, you understand. We'll have to discuss this internally."

"I would expect nothing less," Andrei said, bowing to the king. "We'll find quarters in a local inn and wait your decision, then?"

I was too flabbergasted to think, let alone speak. I stood there dumbfounded.

King Malaky motioned their dismissal.

The Wyranth left together. They walked with heads held high and smug grins plastered on their faces. The Rislandians didn't appear to be happy at all. King Malaky's brows drew together, enhancing the wrinkles in his sallow face. Others shot guarded glances in my direction.

If the Wyranth had intended this as some sort of psychological ploy, it had worked. The guards closed the doors behind them.

King Malaky visibly relaxed.

"The gall of them," Princess Reina said.

"It's almost certainly a ploy," Mr. du Gearsmith said. "Ms. von Monocle, no offense, is in no way a strategic value compared to an airship."

I placed my hands on my hips. "Gee, thanks."

King Malaky attempted to stand, clutching tightly onto the armrest of his throne. A servant rushed to his side to help him up. "I'm afraid this has all been far too laborious for me today with my illness. I need to rest." He looked me in the eye. "Zaira, I value you as a person, and so does this kingdom. Don't forget that. It would make our fight a lot easier to have an airship again, but I would never want you to do something this extreme to retrieve it. We'll find another way."

The servant led King Malaky to a curtain behind the throne, allowing him to exit. Princess Reina stood, and stepped before me. "I'm sorry, Zaira. You shouldn't have to deal with those rats playing mind games with us. It's not right." She moistened her lips and then followed her father out.

Mr. du Gearsmith stepped down from the dais, straightening his suit. "Who would have thought a letter pronouncing your inheritance of an airship would lead to this, hmm?"

It was funny, but I couldn't bring myself to laugh. Did the Iron Emperor really value me this highly? He'd asked me for my hand in marriage before on two occasions, taking great risk to do so. He'd eerily told me he would be asking me three times total, which by this Andrei's proclamation was coming true. I had the feeling if I declined this time, it would be bad—not just for me, but for

Rislandia. But I couldn't be *that* important. Was he obsessed with me? Could Rislandia use this to their advantage?

Mr. du Gearsmith's eyes softened. "Poor child. You're stunned. Diplomatic negations don't usually take this dramatic of a turn, I assure you. This is a strange scenario historians will posit for years to come. Why don't you get some rest? I'm sure King Malaky will want to discuss this with you tomorrow."

What was there to discuss? I couldn't accept the offer. I shook my head to clear my thoughts. "Yeah, that sounds like a good idea." I glanced at the servant who ushered me in. "Would you mind walking me back to my apartment? I don't feel like being alone right now."

The servant nodded and led the way.

CHAPTER 6

THE DAY'S EVENTS left me exhausted.

It was still late afternoon when I returned to my apartment, but it may as well have been late at night. I might have finally lost my patience for paperwork and meetings. Every fiber of my being wanted to get out of this city and back into the sky.

I'd gotten used to the hum of the *Liliana's* engines during my sleep. My apartment had a hushed silence to it by contrast. As I ascended the steps, the quietness unnerved me.

My apartment stood in a row of more than a dozen like it, but I rarely talked to my neighbors. None appeared to be around at the moment.

I'd never felt so lonely when I lived by myself in Plainsroad Village. I had work to do, and my neighbors looked out for me. City life wasn't for me.

I jiggled the key in my lock and opened the door, lost in thoughts about how my old life had been, and what might have been if I still had my airship. When I shut the door behind me, I finally looked into my main room.

A man sat on the couch.

I should have noticed, been more vigilant. Of all the times for me to let my guard slip, why did it have to be now? This marked the second time someone had broken into my apartment since I'd lived here, and worse, the second time a Wyranth had.

The man who sat on my couch, hands folded in his lap as if he belonged there, no care in the world, was Andrei from the Wyranth ambassadorial delegation.

"Hello, Zaira," he said.

Despite the strangeness of the situation, I found I wasn't surprised to find him here.

Having gone to the king's court earlier in the day, I didn't have my weapon on me. I'd hidden my pistol in a drawer to the left, under a framed mirror. I inched my way over there. "I'd ask what you're doing in my apartment, but I already know what you want to say. I'm not going to do it."

"Hear me out, first." His eyes bored into me.

I reached the cabinet, facing Andrei still and reaching behind me to open the drawer. "No, let's start with something else." I grabbed the gun, feeling the hilt of the pistol in my hands, its heavy metallic weight a comfort. Safe. I raised it and pointed it at Andrei. "Tell me who you really are."

Andrei grinned at me. If he feared my gun, he didn't show it. "Always quick on your feet. I like that about you," he said. He glanced down at himself. "I'm going to grab a device in my pocket. It won't harm you. It's not a weapon. But it will answer your question."

Was this another trick? How could I be certain? I could always shoot him if something went wrong. I nodded.

He reached into his pocket and produced a strange metal control with coils and a pulsing light on it. He turned a knob on the device and the light blinked faster before slowly fading out.

I'd been concentrating on the device, and when I looked up to meet Andrei's eyes, I saw it wasn't Andrei at all, but Ivan, the Iron Emperor himself.

Now that his face changed, I could see he had the same wiry form, but he wore clothes that padded his appearance to make him look bulkier. His facial features were stronger than they had been as Andrei, but the eyes were the same. "How?" I breathed.

"It's called a changeling net. You see, I've been working with scientists who are proposing the wildest ideas you can imagine. It's the only way I'm going to be able to compete with Rislandia's resources if we have a prolonged engagement." He grinned. "Which I hope we won't." He placed the device control back in his pocket, and when his hand came out of it, he had the same small rock he had been fidgeting with before.

"You use that to sneak around so no one can recognize you," I said.

Ivan nodded. "Very astute. I'm sure you were trying to piece together how I could walk around Rislandia unescorted and unnoticed. Of course, I couldn't betray my advantage until the time was right."

"Why now?" I asked, moving for a chair across from him. I kept my gun trained on him.

"I want to show you the seriousness of my efforts. Rislandia does not stand a chance against what's coming. My offer of peace is a generous one."

His eyes locked with mine. So intense, so beautiful in many ways, but on the vilest being I could imagine.

I tiptoed closer to him. A foolish move. He could have grabbed the gun from me and then I'd be in really dire straits. But he hadn't shown any inclination toward physically harming me thus far. It was a gamble.

Ivan raised a brow, accenting his smug features.

I slapped him across the face with my free hand.

My palm connected hard, with a loud *clap*. Toby ran from the sound, scurrying back into my bedroom.

Ivan didn't move, didn't flinch. No reaction save for staring at me as he always did. His cheek turned bright red in the shape of my palm and fingers. I'd gotten him good, why didn't he react?

Moments passed, and he raised a hand to touch his cheek. "I suppose you think I deserve such treatment."

"You've murdered thousands of Rislandians and destroyed our lands, all for what?"

"I shan't spend time justifying the war for you, but I assure you, for my people's survival, it is a necessity," Ivan said. He stroked his cheek and then dropped his hand.

I grit my teeth. He made me so angry. "Worse, you lied to me. You told me I needed to go find giants across the ocean." I motioned wildly to the northwest. "And then you set your troops on my country while I was gone."

"We've been over this," Ivan said. "It wasn't my intention. I truly wanted to find more giants' blood to satiate my troops. The serum I'd developed left them with withdrawal symptoms that have driven them quite mad. We're still dealing with the problems now. I hadn't anticipated finding more giants in Rislandian territory for the production. Now, the problem has renewed."

I plopped down in the chair across from him, keeping the gun in my hand. "And I suppose you want me to go on another expedition on your behalf?"

Ivan laughed. "Only to Wyranth. We can get our soldiers under control, but you are far more valuable somewhere you can be close to me."

I felt my cheeks growing hot from his words. I didn't want to react like that. "Why?"

"I told you, I want you to marry me."

"Yes, but *why*? There have to be prettier girls among the Wyranth. My political capital with the Rislandians isn't what you think." I was downright useless in recent weeks, but I didn't need to tell him that.

"I can't answer your question now. I'd need you to come to Wyranth with me. Believe me, it's important, or I wouldn't be persisting in this matter. Remember, this will be the last time I request your hand in marriage."

Those words loomed in the room, heavy.

It might have been the one honest thing he'd ever said to me. But I had to remember all of this could still be a feint or mind game. What did he want with me? I breathed in through my nose, inclining my head. "I'm afraid I'm going to have to decline your offer in marriage. I'm spoken for."

A little concern flashed on Ivan's face, but it quickly faded into his calculated impassiveness. "You've been married since we last met?"

"Well, no." I didn't need to explain myself. What was I doing?

"Then the possibility still awaits. And before you say more, let's talk about the importance of the airship to your kingdom." He twisted the stone in his hand. "The airship is the bane of my people's existence, of course. But with anti-airship artillery, it's not as big of an advantage as you might imagine. True, you can transport items or people in a hurry, but there's a limit."

He leaned back against my couch cushion. "The real advantage lies in psychology. When my people see an airship in the sky, they panic. It causes disruption, chaos amongst my ranks. On the flip side, your people react with raised morale. The combination has turned the tide in many battles over the years. Something about the hulking presence in the sky makes its effect impossible to replicate otherwise. You need your airship in the sky for Rislandia to succeed. Am I correct?"

I didn't want to confirm anything to him, but he knew the tactics better than I did. It at least made sense. "Sure."

"And therefore to restore your kingdom to hope, even if peace is reached where we can agree on a new border, having it in the sky would be invaluable."

"You're not saying anything I don't already know," I said.

Ivan smiled. "No, but I'm making you think about it. The airship is more valuable than you to this kingdom, this is true. But you are more valuable to my empire. I know why your airship isn't able to take flight. I have the answers your engineers seek."

"How can we possibly trust you?"

He pressed a hand to his chest. "Your unbelief brings me great distress. I am a man of my word, Zaira."

The way he said my name sent shivers down my spine.

In a lot of ways, he was right. The airship did matter to Rislandia a lot more than my participation here. With the king ill, and everyone on edge, we needed a decisive victory. And our troops could use a break. If we could achieve an armistice...

What was I thinking? Could I trust him?

Ivan stood. "I see I've given you a lot to think about." He retrieved the changeling net controller from his hand and turned the dial again. The harder features of "Andrei" returned to his face, though his eyes remained the same. "Sleep on it. My delegation will be here to wait for you. It would be regrettable for your answer to my *final* proposal to be the wrong one." He took a few steps toward my door, ignoring that I still had a gun trained on him. Once at the door, he stopped and looked back over his shoulder. "Oh, and don't bother having your people search for me. I will be long gone before you can sound an alarm."

He exited the door, leaving me standing there, stunned.

Toby shuffled back from the bedroom when Ivan shut the door, and came sniffing around my ankles.

"What do I do, Toby? This is insanity," I said.

It truly was. I couldn't believe Ivan was so dead set on me of all people, and more, I couldn't believe he had a proposal worth listening to. But I was spoken for. How could I leave Ethan? Especially when I couldn't even talk to him about the matter? He was gone on a mission, and I I'd betrayed him for even sparing a thought toward Ivan's proposal.

If Ivan's intended to rattle me, he'd succeeded in his efforts. But what else? Perhaps both leaders were right—I should take some time to rest before determining anything. This was all too strange of a situation to make decisions while in a frenzied emotional state.

"Alright, Toby. Let's feed you and then go speak with King Malaky," I said.

Toby chirped in contentment.

CHAPTER 7

"HE SOUNDED SINCERE," I said, sitting at a round table with King Malaky, my father, Talyen, and Mr. du Gearsmith.

Lunch was set before us, a quiche with salad, but none of us had touched our food. The unsettling news of the Iron Emperor's presence in our city had killed our appetites.

"I still can't believe the city watch searched all through the night and found no trace of him," King Malaky said. "I appreciate you coming to me right away over the matter. How could he be so close, and yet slip through our hands?"

"I told you, he has a device which can mask his appearance," I said.

King Malaky sighed. Though he didn't look nearly as gaunt as he had the prior day, he still had sweat beading on his brow and a pale sickness to him. My father suggested he handle the meeting instead, but the king insisted on being present.

"Don't stress yourself too much on the matter, your Majesty," Mr. du Gearsmith said. "If such technology truly exists, it presents an incredible advantage for him. He could be anyone."

Everyone looked at each other, suspicions heightened.

I shook my head. "No, not anyone. It's not a perfect device. His general build was about the same as I remembered him being, but he padded his suit to appear bulkier. The device only seemed to impact his facial contours, and it couldn't change his eyes. There are limits to what he can do, but he can still hide amongst any people in anonymity."

"Handy," my father said. "I could have certainly used the device on several of my missions."

Talyen smiled. "Fortunately, you don't need to anymore."

"Let's focus," King Malaky said. "This presents quite a conundrum for us. As much as I hate to admit it, the Iron Emperor is right. Not only about the fighting. It needs to end soon, before our men give in from pure exhaustion. But he's also correct regarding the airship and its meaning to Rislandia. Being able to have the airship flying again would be a much-needed boost for both our military and civilians." He winced, as if the words pained him, before turning to the side and coughing. "Excuse me."

The table quieted while King Malaky regained his composure.

My father took a sip of water. "You can't seriously be entertaining the idea that Zaira marry that fiend," he said.

I hadn't heard my father so defensive of me before. It filled me with both pride and anger. I liked him caring about me, but I was an adult. I could make my own decisions.

"I could never ask that of her," King Malaky said.

And yet the tone in his voice was clear—he wanted to. The airship meant too much to Rislandia. It meant too much to *me*. What good would it do for me if I were married and trapped in the Wyranth Empire without the ability to fly the skies? Would someone else get my ship? I would lose everything in this scenario.

"We have to consider the long-term future, your Majesty," Mr. du Gearsmith said. "If the Iron Emperor weds Zaira, and the fighting persists, then what? She becomes our enemy? Baron von Monocle is a symbol to our people as much as the airship is."

"The object would be to ensure the fighting doesn't continue," King Malaky said. He shook his head. "I can't fathom granting them the lands in the south, however. Those people are our people as much as the ones here or north."

"We shouldn't give them an inch," my father said.

Mr. du Gearsmith dabbed his lips with a napkin. "There are costs and benefits to every situation. This battle has waged with the Wyranth for how long now?"

"Since they overran the Tyndree kingdom and turned their focus on us," my father said.

"Tyndree... my mother was from there, wasn't she?" I asked.

My father nodded, his face growing solemn. "I wish we could have provided those people more help, but at least we got your mother out of there."

There were a lot more puzzle pieces to this whole mess than I could visualize. I recalled my first meeting with Ivan. He'd mentioned my mother. Did she have something to do with this? Was there more history here? The only problem was, no one much cared *why* Ivan wanted what he did. No one other than me. The mystery was mine alone.

"So, what do we do?" I asked.

Everyone at the table looked at me. Had I spoken out of turn? We needed to come to some conclusion. Ivan and the Wyranth were either mucking with our minds, or this was a real solution.

Despite all the subterfuge, I found I believed Ivan. The way he laid everything out... he had been honest with me the whole time. He posed what the problems were, told me what he wanted, and it was all very open. Did I distrust him simply because of his identity? I frowned, thinking about it.

"We do whatever you think is best, Zaira," King Malaky said. "Were I in your position, I would ignore the offer. We would find another way. But... if he does hold the secrets to airship flight, it is something to consider."

"Do you think he's telling the truth?" I asked, looking King Malaky in the eye. A year ago, I would have been frightened out of my mind to gaze into the eyes of a king like an equal. Today, it had become commonplace.

King Malaky made a somber expression as he considered. "The Wyranth are ruthless. They've tried to assassinate me. They succeeded in assassinating my father. However, when I have spoken to their diplomats, I never came to the conclusion they were lying to me. Withholding information, possibly. It's what makes this so strange. What on earth could he want with you?"

That was the ten thousand gold coin question. I could have taken it as a slight, but it didn't make sense to me either. Ivan said he had a reason, but I would have to agree and go with the Wyranth to find out what it was. Maddening. I almost wanted to say yes just to learn the truth.

But that wasn't a good reason for me to take a rash action. Helping the kingdom, on the other hand, could be.

What about Ethan, though?

My heart lurched in my chest. I thought of him so little ever since Ivan had laid this proposal on me. Ethan should be foremost on my mind. At some point, Ethan would probably ask for my hand in marriage, or at least I hoped he would. We hadn't committed to anything. We hadn't even discussed our relationship much. Beyond the knights who helped Ethan with our date, James Gentry catching us kissing a few times, and some of the airship crew doing the same, few people knew how close we'd become.

If he were in my position...

His face popped into my mind. Dark eyes with a serious loving tenderness, looking down at me after we'd just kissed. *"I serve the king first,"* he'd said, one of the last things I'd heard from him before he left on his mission.

He would always serve king and country first. I would too, for that matter. And I could tell, despite his words and coyness, King Malaky hoped I would follow through with the Iron Emperor's wish. I wasn't a bad asset to lose if it meant gaining an airship.

I gripped onto the tablecloth, needing something to hold. The whole thought process hurt me to my core, giving me a sinking feeling like none other. But it also gave me pride. I was Rislandian. I would put my country before my feelings.

"I'll do it," I managed to squeak out.

"Pardon?" my father asked, a horrified expression crossing his face.

"Zaira, you can't be serious," Talyen said.

"We should discuss this further," Mr. du Gearsmith said.

Everyone stared at me in shocked silence for a long time.

"Let's hear her out," King Malaky said.

"The airship is what's most important, and so is ending this war. We've done what we can. It's time to bring peace back to Rislandia so we can rebuild. Besides, I can work from the inside of the Wyranth Empire to make sure this sort of thing never happens again. It's best for everyone." *Except me.*

"That's preposterous, Zaira. You're my daughter!" my father said.

I met his eyes directly. "I am. And you would do the same if our situations were reversed."

My father clamped his lips tight.

Talyen sighed. "She's your daughter, all right. And you know what happens when *you* decide upon something, no matter how foolish."

My father huffed.

Mr. du Gearsmith tried to keep calm on his face, but I could tell he was displeased. "We may be able to take further advantage of this situation if this pleases your majesty," he said to King Malaky as if I weren't there.

King Malaky nodded.

Mr. du Gearsmith cleared his throat. "Dr. von Gunsmith mentioned he's been working on a micro-camera, one to take photographs but at a fraction of the size of a regular device. Zaira could conceal one, and she can act as an informant to us."

"You're not only telling my daughter to go marry the Iron Emperor, but you're asking her to be a spy while she's there? You're going to get her head lobbed off!" my father spat.

"Please, Theodore," King Malaky said. "These are desperate times. Zaira has proved herself competent."

Those words made me perk up. "Thank you," I said.

"It's not right," my father said under his breath.

"No, it's not," I said. "But given the way fate has turned events in this world, sometimes we have to do what's painful to ourselves to help the cause. You know that better than anyone else."

My father quieted.

"Then it's settled," I said, regretting every word I was speaking. My whole body screamed *no!* to me, and yet I had to do my duty. For King Malaky and for Rislandia. *For steam and country,* I thought. "I'm doing it."

Mr. du Gearsmith inclined his head. "I'll inform the Wyranth delegation."

"I'll want someone to come with me to help and act as protection. Someone to watch my back in case things go wrong," I said. The wheels turned in my head, formulating a plan. Would I go through with the wedding after I went down there? I didn't know, but I had to go—one step at a time.

"Of course," King Malaky said.

"I want Marina du Willet to join me," I said.

King Malaky looked around the table. "Any objections?"

"Didn't she used to be a Wyranth spy?" Mr. du Gearsmith asked.

"I trust her implicitly," I said.

"I would feel much better with her looking out for Zaira," Talyen said.

King Malaky nodded. "Then she will join you. Thank you, Zaira. Your sacrifice is one of the most touching examples of loyalty I could have ever imagined. I would never command you to do such a thing. I will make sure your name is revered in this land."

"Thank you, your Majesty," I said, my mouth going dry.

It was a sacrifice all right. I hoped it would pay off, and that it wouldn't be in vain.

CHAPTER 8

MR. DU GEARSMITH drafted a formal letter, conveying my acceptance of the Wyranth proposal to marry the emperor in exchange for vital information on the airship technology to make the ship fly again. I would personally verify the airship information to be true before signing my life away in earnest, and Marina would ensure the information made it safely back to Rislandia when the ceremony occurred.

All parties were in agreement, but we still needed to be vigilant to ensure the Wyranth kept their end of the bargain. I didn't get the sense Ivan lied about his intentions, but one could never tell. He was the type to be *technically* honest, but to also withhold some vital information that made his "truth" a deception nonetheless.

It was for me to make sure Rislandia got what it needed. That was my purpose, even if the rest of my life ahead of me would be a dreary one.

And what would I do? Would I be locked up in the Wyranth castle all day, a prisoner as an empress? Empress Zaira von

Monocle. I'd never thought the title before. I didn't want it. I was happy with being called baron or baronette.

But I'd made my decision. I couldn't back out now. It was best to forget my adventuring life and get this ordeal behind me. I could find some way to contribute to the world from the Wyranth Empire.

The Wyranth delegation agreed to give me three days to get ready. I didn't have much to pack. Most of my clothes and belongings were already mobile, so I could quickly be ready for airship travel. I didn't have many friends outside my family, Ethan, and James, leaving few people to whom I needed to say my goodbyes. I visited some of the airship crew who still resided in the city. Some of the commandos had been reassigned to infantry duty, needed for the intense battles against our southern enemy. Others went back home to assist with their cities' rebuilding efforts.

I had tea with Dr. du Clockhand and her husband, Trevor. They'd recently married, and Dr. du Clockhand beamed proudly to let me know she had a baby on the way. Our goodbye was filled with tears, smiles, congratulations, condolences.

Seeing them only sapped my energy. Dr. du Clockhand reminded me of what I once had—trips across continents, strange creatures, adventure, a purpose. I'd have to find it again, somehow.

Mr. du Gearsmith introduced me to his scientist friend, who showed me the workings of the micro-camera. It was easy to use. I wouldn't be able to see the photographs myself—I'd have to take it back to his lab—but he assured me it could take a hundred and five pictures. Simple enough. I thanked the scientist and Mr. du Gearsmith for their time and went about my business.

The main problem I had to deal with was Toby. Could I bring him to live in the Wyranth Empire? He would be so upset if I left him, but I didn't want to risk the possibility that Ivan wouldn't want a pet around. Nor did I feel comfortable with Toby in enemy territory. There was too much that could go wrong. I'd miss the little ferret, but what else could I do?

I asked around if people would be willing to take him in. Finally, Talyen relented, saying it would be nice to have a pet around for Lilly. I warned Talyen about ferrets around the baby—she would have to be careful until Lilly grew to be older. Talyen agreed. It was a great relief. Toby would be among family.

My final day in Rislandia city came. Everything was set up the way I wanted it to be, but my heart felt emptier than ever. I had hoped Ethan would return from his mission, so I could at least get one last conversation with him. I was betraying him, despite our never firming the details of what we expected from our budding relationship. But it had to be done. This was my duty.

I penned him a letter, trying not to shake as I wrote.

Ethan,

By the time you get this letter, I will be gone forever.

Events transpired since you left and the Wyranth Emperor has asked for my hand in marriage. Absurd, I know, but as a trade, he promised to give Rislandia the information needed to get the airship off the ground again. Our airship means so much to this country. King Malaky seems to think this is of utmost importance.

But I know I don't need to explain myself to you. You're the only person to ever truly understand me. You get my drive, my need to serve. You're the same way. When we parted, we talked about duty and how it would take us away from each other. I understood it would be one of many partings for the future, and though my heart reaches for you, I had to be able to let you go.

This is much harder because it's permanent. You and I together is a new thing. We haven't truly had time to solidify what we meant to each other. I implore you, don't fret about what could have been. Just know my heart is yours. I love you, Ethan, and that will always hold.

For now, I must do my duty. Find someone nice, who can be there for you and doesn't have her own duties as I do. I know it will be hard. It's hard for me too.

Goodbye.

Love,

Zaira von Monocle

The letter seemed so inadequate. I wanted to say so much more to him. To tell him I loved him over and over. To kiss his face. What I wouldn't give to hold him one more time. Tears streaked down my face and dripped on the parchment. I turned away so more wouldn't fall and smudge the ink. I hoped he would understand. I truly did.

A knock came at the door. I forced myself to calm down, wiped my eyes, and opened the door. The Wyranth delegation stood at my doorstep, along with my father and Mr. du Gearsmith.

"Are you ready?" my father asked.

I met his eyes to let him know I understood. I felt much the same way.

One of the Wyranth servants gathered my belongings, placing them in the back of an enclosed cart attached to a horseless carriage. The engine was on, exhaust blowing from the top of it.

The wind blew the flags around the capital to the north. It kept pushing my hair into my face.

Mr. du Gearsmith took my hand. "The king sends his regrets he cannot personally see you off. His health is... less than satisfactory, and he needs to rest. You understand."

I nodded.

"You're a treasure, Ms. von Monocle," Mr. du Gearsmith said. "The kingdom will be less without you, and we appreciate what you're doing for us."

I nodded again.

I'd already cried my eyes out. They must have been red, my face puffy and a mess. At least I hadn't gone through the ritual of applying my face. Eyeliner streaking would have made matters worse. I hadn't been able to bear the thought of prettying myself for this foul journey. I hated that this was the last way my father would see me.

My father brought me into a tight embrace. He leaned in close. "You can always change your mind, Zaira. We will come for you."

"I know," I whispered.

"I love you more than anything. I think this is a foolish idea, but you're doing it for the right reasons. That's what's important. You're a great example to anyone fighting. And hopefully, the fighting will be over soon."

"I hope so too."

We held quiet for a moment, the wind picking up again. Then, I pulled back from him. I couldn't wait here any longer. If I did, he would try to talk me out of going, and I couldn't have that. The kingdom needed its airship back, even if I wouldn't be the one to captain her anymore.

I met my father's eyes once more, but I didn't say goodbye. I couldn't. I would see him again. I would do whatever it took to make sure Ivan stopped this war on my people.

It didn't feel like much of a purpose, trying to bend the ear of the Iron Emperor. But it would have to be enough for now. I was Zaira von Monocle, and I had to save the lives of Rislandian soldiers.

Whatever it took.

The Wyranth escorted me into the carriage. I sat, the metal door closing, locking me in, confining me even as the carriage took off and air rushed across my face.

Marina sat across from me, a beautiful woman in her own right, with dark hair and a strong chin. She was my best friend.

She reached over and took my hand, squeezing it. "You have to be the bravest person I've ever met," she said.

"Or the stupidest," I said.

We didn't say more as we sped down the cobblestone streets. The city guard let us out the main gates, and we took to the road, heading for the plains of central Rislandia. I turned back to see the Crystal Spire fading in the distance.

CHAPTER 9

IT WAS LATE afternoon by the time we made it past Plainsroad Village. The whole town still lay in waste from the earlier Wyranth invasion. No one had the resources to rebuild. The former town was close to our infantry line between Greenhorne and Loveridge, where the war had its heaviest battles.

No one wanted to risk resettling, not yet. I hoped with my work in the Wyranth Empire, I could help to bring peace of mind to people who might live here. It would be nice for Rislandia to be safe again.

We had to drive slowly, as we crossed large holes created by explosions in the road, along with other debris that had settled, turning our once smooth travel way into a bumpy mess. No one seemed to be anywhere around us, until we came to a small patch of trees.

A cart had flipped on the side of the road. A few merchants stood around it, trying their hardest to turn it back over. It blocked enough of the path forward that we had to stop. Our driver, a Wyranth delegate named Ando, stepped out of the car.

"Can we be of assistance?" he asked one of the merchants, a haggard-looking man with patches of long, whiskery hair on his face.

The whiskery man smiled, revealing a lack of front teeth. "No, we're about to be just fine," he said.

Guns appeared in the hands of his companions. Three pistols pointed straight at us, along with a rifle held by a man behind the cart. The whiskery man opened a sack. "All of your coin in here. And drop your cart, whatever you're carrying. We'll let you go on, generously. A toll to continue onto the line, you see. It's dangerous out here on the road."

"That it is," Ando said. "You would do well to let us pass."

Whiskers laughed. "You hear that boys? I think they want us to show them we're serious."

He turned back to his friends, laughing with them. When he turned back around, he had a gun in his hand, and he pointed it at Ando. "We mean business, friends."

"No!" I shouted.

The bandit fired the gun.

The bullet grazed past Ando's ear, a little splatter of blood coming off of the Wyranth. He grabbed his ear and yelped.

Whiskers went down, hands grasping his chest.

I turned to the side. Marina had a rifle pointed out of the carriage, smoke wafting from it. "Get down, Baronette," she said.

I ducked as bullets came blasting into the carriage. I had a pistol holstered on my hip, one I hadn't used in several months, but I wasn't afraid of it. I produced the gun, trying to get a clear view of my targets.

Four bandits appeared in front of us, matching our numbers. Our position held much more exposure than our enemies, who took care to find concealment. Two of the bandits hid behind a tree while the other two used their overturned cart as cover.

Ando rushed for the carriage to put it between him and the bandits, but as he did, bullets pelted him in the back. Our driver was down. It left one Wyranth plus Marina and myself. The remaining Wyranth, Melker, I hadn't spoken with during the journey so far. What would we do if he died as well? Would the Wyranth believe we were complacent in their deaths? The bandits didn't know it, but they were creating a more precarious situation than a simple robbery.

Melker had been smart enough to duck. He had a pistol in his hand, and appeared to be savvy with it. "Protect von Monocle at all costs," he said to Marina. "The Iron Emperor would be quite angry if she weren't to survive."

"I'm trying," Marina said. She fired her rifle toward the cart.

It was a standoff. But who would run out of bullets first? Several more projectiles zinged in our direction. The bandits didn't seem too concerned about conserving their ammunition.

I wished we had our commandos with us. While Marina could hold her own, my team would be able to handle this incident swiftly. Was there a way to get to our infantry line? The bandits wouldn't set up so close to those who could fire back. I found myself at a loss for ideas.

We exchanged more volleys of shots. I didn't dare raise my head, so I fired blindly at the enemy.

"Save your bullets," Marina said. "You'll do no good like that."

"Okay," I said.

The windshield of our carriage shattered. Melker yelped in pain.

"Are you all right?" I asked, unable to see where he was from my position hiding behind the first row of seats.

"Glass got lodged in my neck. Hurts," he said. He breathed through his teeth, cringing in pain. But we couldn't do anything about it right now.

"There has to be some way out of this," I said.

Marina fired her rifle. The gurgle of someone struggling to breathe reached my ears. "One more down," Marina said. "At least it's even now."

No shots rang out for a long while, both sides sizing each other up and waiting for an opportunity.

"You'd better come out," shouted one of the bandits. "We won't hurt you if you surrender."

'Yeah, we just want money," another said.

That wouldn't be an option. We couldn't let these men take all of our things. Besides, they would attack the next unsuspecting group who came along the road. I wished we had something we could use to our advantage, but I still couldn't conceive of anything. Even one of us getting killed at this point would be too many. We couldn't risk it.

"I think we should surrender," I said in a low tone.

"You?" Marina asked in disbelief.

"I mean it. We don't need our belongings. It's not worth it."

"I doubt they'll let us go. They know we'll tell the military of their whereabouts," Marina said.

I scrunched my nose. "Yeah. I hadn't thought of that."

"That's why you have me around," Marina said.

"The best plan would be to stall until one of your army vehicles comes down the road. It is only a matter of time, yes?" Melker asked.

I bit my lip, considering. "I'm not sure. We don't have a lot of units we can move back and forth right now."

"Let's hope they do."

As if on cue, another motor sounded on the road back from the direction which we came. It slowed as it came to the area where our car and the overturned cart blocked the road.

The bandits fired at them immediately, but whoever was in the carriage returned fire just as quickly. Another bandit went down.

I poked my head up to see what was going on. The remaining two fled into the trees. I glanced behind us.

It wasn't our army who'd come to save the day, but more Wyranth. A second car of the delegation that had been in King Malaky's chambers. Guards. They had guns.

"I told you should have waited for us, Melker," one of the Wyranth said.

Melker sat back up into his seat in the carriage, glancing over his shoulder. "Should we go after them?"

Marina shook her head. "No. Let's continue on. We don't need to risk more casualties to stop two ruffians."

Melker nodded. He moved over to the driver's seat. He frowned as he spotted Ando's body beside the car. "He served the Empire well," he said under his breath.

Then, he started the carriage. The motor rumbled, and we bounced down the road.

CHAPTER 10

THE REST OF the journey proved uneventful. Our soldiers stopped us at the line and surveyed our travel papers. We then rode in quiet tension between the Rislandian line and the Wyranth's, but the opposing army didn't fire upon us. They, too, inspected our papers when we arrived, but let us pass without any problems.

We drove through Loveridge, a town I hadn't been to since my first flight with the airship. My heart grew heavy with longing for a return to those simpler days. I thought I'd been overwhelmed at the time. Now older, I wished I'd had longer to enjoy it, even the more difficult moments. I already missed Talyen, Harkerpal, Colwell, and the others. Would I see them again? I truly hoped so.

Once along the drive into Wyranth territory, the frightening aspects of the ride dulled. We passed into the rolling hills of the enemy empire, several small villages along the way, but none appeared distinct from another. I'd been in this region once when we raided the Wyranth capital to rescue my father. Marina had been with me then.

I turned to her. She stared out into the distance. Did she miss her time among her people here? Ever since that time, she'd shown only the utmost loyalty to me. I'd had an impact on her, if I'd done nothing else with my life.

"You okay?" I asked, sensing unease from her.

"I wasn't sure I'd ever be back here again," Marina said. "It's strange. Doesn't feel like home anymore."

"Did you grow up in the capital?" I asked.

She shook her head. "In one of the small villages we passed."

"You didn't say anything."

"Not much to say. The secret police pried me from my parents at a young age when they saw I had aptitude as a spy. They took me into one of their training programs."

I'd never known this about her past before. We'd been working together for over a year, and I'd never found the occasion to ask her. Part of me felt guilty for that, but I found it hard to pry into her life. Marina probably didn't enjoy the reminder that she had once been an agent of this evil empire. "That's crazy, being torn from your family."

She shrugged. "No worse than your upbringing."

I'd lost my mother to disease, and my father always galivanted away on adventures. I'd been left alone in a very real way. I supposed the only difference between her and me is I learned to farm while she learned to kill. "True," I said. "Did you ever speak to them again?"

"Once or twice," Marina said. "They didn't feel much like family afterward. The agency was my family. I'm... not sure I want to run into any of them again."

"I understand," I said, though I didn't. We paused the conversation for several moments, before I turned to her again. "Thank you for coming with me. I know it must be difficult for you to leave Rhys."

"It's a mission," Marina said. "Nothing I haven't done before."

Her lips tightened, her expression guarded.

"Yeah, but you weren't with someone before, were you?" I asked.

"I had a beau when I was in the agency. But Rhys will wait for me or he won't. He understands the risks of being with me."

That hit all too close to home, as it made me think about Ethan again. I shifted in my seat. "What happened to him? Your beau, that is."

Marina shrugged again.

I imagined that was why she was acting so strange about coming to the Wyranth capital. She didn't want to face her past relationships. It made sense now.

Before we could continue the conversation, we came over the peak of nearby hills, descending into a walled city, with bright lights radiating from it, the early evening upon us. A dark shadow of Devil's Mountain loomed in the background. We'd reached the Wyranth capital.

The city stood, a hulking monstrosity, large towers peering down on us, stone walls giving it a cold and uninviting atmosphere, at least from my perspective. Compared to Rislandia City's palace and the Crystal Spire, the Wyranth capital had a dark ugliness to it. The main gates to the city were well lit, illuminating a large opening that swallowed this main road into its clutches.

The entrance's design looked much like Rislandia City's, and I recalled stories of the builders of the two major castles being from the same group of travelers hundreds of years ago.

Melker slowed the carriage as we approached the city, and we came to a stop at the gates.

One Wyranth soldier stood, checking papers of those entering the capital. Their security had increased since our knights broke into the city to rescue us a year ago. The guard let the carriage in front of us go, and then it was our turn.

Melker greeted his compatriot with a salute, and the guard returned the gesture. Two more guards stood at the gates, one on each side. Where some of the Wyranth's metallic, pointed helmets reflected the gas lamps, these guards had a metallic shine throughout their bodies.

"You're clear," the guard said, handing Melker's documents back.

Melker pulled forward. When we came closer, I saw the two shining guards weren't humans at all. Faceless metal contraptions glared down at me. The light reflected off of them because they were composed of the same materials as the helmets themselves. Each guard held a rifle and stood still.

"Are those statues supposed to scare people off?" I asked.

Melker laughed. "They aren't statues. They're automatons."

"Automatons?" Marina asked. "Unnatural."

"Perhaps," Melker said. "But they are much easier to control than regular human troops. Especially those who were addicted to the serum."

We putted slowly through the streets in our carriage, bouncing on the cobblestones inside, much as we had in Rislandia City.

Most of the shops had their doors and shutters closed, leaving the streets dark. Some apartments had lights on. A local tavern bustled with people, several standing outside waiting for a chance to go inside. But what shocked me was that every three blocks stood another pair of automatons. They kept the entire city secured via these mechanical creatures.

When had the Wyranth invented these? I had never so much as heard of them before. It must have been a recent build.

Recalling my micro-camera, I pulled it from my satchel, careful to keep it out of the view of Melker. I snapped a few photographs. Hopefully, they would turn out well enough with the light of the street lamps.

We came upon a town square, with a large statue of what appeared to be Ivan, but in clothes from a hundred years prior—ruffled shirt and a tri-cornered hat. Flowers surrounded the station, leading to a green lawn area, causing a circle in the road. No one stood in the square in the evening, save for two more automaton guards. "Is that a statue of the Iron Emperor?"

"His great- great-grandfather," Melker said.

"Ah," I said. I didn't know much about Wyranth history.

We circled the statue park and came upon the palace. A gate hung in front of us, and two human guards pulled it open to allow us entry. I'd not seen the palace from the exterior before, having only entered from underground dungeons as my captors had escorted me. It had large columns supporting an overhanging roof that stretched several feet from the main building, creating a sort of veranda, if something so opulent could be called by such a mundane word.

We parked in front, and I stepped out onto a tile mosaic.

More guards greeted us, leading the way into the palace where I'd been once before. I wasn't here in a state of confusion this time, but could fully appreciate its grandeur. Decorations adorned the hallway—paintings of war heroes, gilded lamps and candelabras, and a long purple rug stretched through the main corridor.

Marina tugged at my arm and whispered in my ear. "Treat every moment as if you're under surveillance. You likely will be."

I nodded as the soldiers escorted us deeper into the palace.

Automaton guards lined the hallways, a pair every few steps. Their mechanical presence provided a creepy atmosphere to the place. Their blank faces stared at me wherever I moved. Goosebumps formed on my arms and neck. Would I have to live with these things?

Ivan rounded a corner, stopping in front of us. Our Wyranth guardians took knees. Both Marina and I stood.

The Iron Emperor stood in a fresh suit, hanging perfectly on his somewhat thin but tall form. His eyes fell upon us. He smiled. "Good. You made it. I was beginning to worry."

"We ran into some trouble along the way, your Eminence," Melker said.

"Oh?" Ivan cocked a brow.

Melker recounted the story of the bandit attack. Ivan's expression turned deadly. "Ando was right to protect your future empress. He will be honored, and his family will receive a reward for his sacrifice. Make sure my herald is aware of this," Ivan said.

"Yes, your Majesty."

Ivan returned his attention to me. "Anything you desire that is within this Empire's ability to grant is yours, Zaira. Do not hesitate to ask. We have a long day tomorrow in which you'll tour the city. Rest well." He smiled.

I forced one back. It wouldn't do me any good to fight right now. "Thank you," I said.

Ivan nodded and took his leave of us.

Melker stood once more when the Iron Emperor departed, turning back to us. "You didn't bow."

"No," I said flatly.

He shook his head, his expression judging me, but he didn't say anything else. "Come, I'll show you to the guest attendants."

Marina and I followed, unsure of what would lay next. All of this was happening so fast, and it was all so strange. I'd gotten myself into a mess, with no one else I could possibly blame, and I had no plan on how to get out of it again.

CHAPTER II

A GOOD NIGHT'S sleep cures a lot of ills, my mother used to tell me when I was a child. Her words proved true again, as I awoke feeling less stressed than the day prior.

The Wyranth servants had fed us, bathed us, and shown us to rooms. The quarters were more comfortable than the guest quarters in King Malaky's palace. A rug on the floor made it so my toes wouldn't get cold in the morning when I first stood.

Ivan disappeared into meetings for the day, allowing me to spend time with Marina and get accustomed to my new Wyranth home. It wasn't as bad as I expected.

Whatever had preoccupied Ivan took him longer than he'd estimated. I spent two more days in the palace, and found myself bored before he finally summoned me.

A small package awaited me at my door, which soured my better mood. It reminded me of the dress Ethan bought me, as it had a similar bow garnishing it. I picked the package up and opened the box nonetheless, finding another dress inside. Had someone told these men I needed clothes?

It was green, pretty, and modest. I couldn't find fault in it, but I also didn't want to wear a gift from the Iron Emperor. If I wanted to rebel, I should wear my standard von Monocle fare, with my red cape flowing behind me.

But as I thought about my situation, making a rebellious gesture like that wouldn't be a great way to start my stay here. Especially as I might have to live in this palace the rest of my days.

After deliberating, I put on the dress, finding it fit me well enough, though a little tightly around the bosom.

Once dressed, I made my way out of the room. I found a servant who ushered me to Ivan's private sitting room, the room where he'd brought me the last time I was in this castle—equally under duress, but in much worse conditions then. He sat by the fire, fixated on a book. He finished whatever passage he read before looking up at me.

"Ah, Zaira," he said. "You look wonderful in the dress. I commissioned the finest tailor in our city to make it for you, in anticipation of your arrival today."

"How long ago did you do that?"

Ivan smiled. "Why, when you first visited us last year."

His words made me shiver. What was wrong with him? How could I even broach the subject without seeming awkward? I had to somehow. I needed to know what made me so special to him. He'd mentioned in Rislandia City he had a good reason, but I couldn't for the life of me figure out what it could be.

"You're wondering why I brought you here, aren't you?" Ivan asked. He had an uncanny way of reading me which almost seemed like he sensed my thoughts. His hand slipped over to one of the end tables where he picked up the stone I'd seen him carrying before, twirling it in his palm.

The stone distracted me. He'd been carrying it so often it must have had some value to him. What could it have been? A keepsake?

"Yeah," I said, moving over to the couch across from him. I helped myself to a seat and smoothed down my dress.

"I suppose since you've agreed to the proposal, you deserve the explanation," he said. "However, it's going to have to wait until later. I booked us a tour around the city so you can get acquainted with your new people, and they can get acquainted with you. We'll also be touring my new war factory. You'll see why it's imperative Rislandia stop fighting us."

I held my tongue, wanting to lash out and tell him we'd fight him until our last breaths, but this wouldn't be the time for theatrics. I had to be patient. A war factory presented a good opportunity. If I could get away from Ivan, even for a little while, I could snap photographs with my micro-camera. Perhaps we could send Marina back sooner rather than later and get my people the information they needed.

As much as I wanted him to tell me the reason for my being here, I could be patient. I had a lot of time, didn't I? "Okay, let's go."

"I'm glad you're so amicable, Zaira. It's a refreshing change from our last meetings. You've grown up," Ivan said, standing, towering over me. He stepped toward the couch and offered his hand.

Could I take it? I stared at his outstretched hand for a moment. He had long fingers, pale skin, clean fingernails. His touch wouldn't hurt me. I gave him my hand.

His touch was warmer than I expected. Part of me imagined he'd be clammy and cold. In truth, he was anything but. His hands were soft, yet his grip was firm. I didn't find myself as repulsed as I wanted to be.

"Our horseless carriage awaits outside," Ivan said, releasing my hand once I'd stood.

We walked side by side through the long palace corridors and past the automatons.

"Do you have to have those in the palace? What if they malfunction?" I asked.

"They're much safer than human guards. A man can rebel for all kinds of reasons. My automatons are safe as long as my commanders don't cause me problems. Less points of possible failure. It's better to run an empire that way."

We reached the main entrance outside. The Wyranth capital appeared more vibrant in the daylight. It was the first time I'd seen the inside of the city's walls at this hour. Buildings stood, painted several different colors ranging from whites to blues and greys. Smoke puffed from some factories in the distance, but the sky was clear back to Devil's Mountain behind us. I glanced upward and around.

"It's a beautiful place," Ivan said.

"Much better than the dungeon," I said.

Ivan laughed as a soldier came around with the carriage. Another opened the door so we could sit in the back. This carriage had a hardtop, with the steamstack protruding through the middle of it. It was claustrophobic compared to the open models I'd ridden in.

"Is Marina going to be joining us?" I asked. The experience had been such a whirlwind so far I'd forgotten to ask for my friend.

"Oh, I made her other plans to meet with my diplomats and verify our airship plans are authentic. Do you need her along with you?" Ivan asked. "If you're more comfortable..."

I shook my head. "She's got important work to do." I had brought her along to be a bodyguard, but Ivan wouldn't let me come to harm.

The driver pressed the aether fuel pedal, and we took off down the street.

As with my first impression of the exterior of the castle, vibrant buildings cluttered the streets with color, often with differently painted frames around the windows to make the houses and shops pop with even more variation. Enough people drove and walked through the streets that it didn't feel empty, but the automatons standing along major intersections still gave the place a strange, looming quality. It was as if there could be trouble in any moment.

"This," Ivan said, pointing out the window of the horseless carriage at a circular building, "is the Wyranth Opera House. Have you heard opera music before?"

I shook my head.

"Oh, the intricacies. Rislandians don't often get the vivid culture we produce. Your country is suppressed by a utilitarian philosophy where art isn't appreciated."

"That's not true," I said.

"Oh?" Ivan raised a brow at me, daring me to prove him wrong.

I didn't have a good retort. I'd certainly spent my life in a utilitarian manner, working the farm and then doing my duty aboard the airship. Even with my ship gone, I'd hardly ventured into anything Ivan would consider cultural. The closest I'd come was my evening date with Ethan, with the meal the knights had prepared. Cooking was artistry, wasn't it?

Ivan looked back out the window, satisfied he was correct. I wanted to slap the smugness from his face. "There's a lot of wonder out there, Zaira. I hope we'll be able to fully explore it together."

What did he mean by that? Before I had a chance to reply, a change in scenery distracted me.

We moved into an industrial district to the west, which looked like it had been built outside the original city walls, though a newer stone wall surrounded this area. Large smokestacks puffed exhaust into the air. The car stopped in front of one of the factories, and Ivan exited the car. Energy radiated from him, a bounce in his step I hadn't seen prior.

The driver opened my door to allow me out. Ivan led me to a large, gated door, reminiscent of one of my barn doors. He pulled open the bar holding it secure, taking more initiative than I had figured he would.

"What's this?" I asked.

"The future," Ivan said.

A large assembly-line factory filled my vision. Metal equipment pressed and forged parts. Piping ran chemicals through their tubes, and a gear-based conveyor moved parts that passed different Wyranth who sat in stations, attaching the various metal parts as they came along.

Freshly minted automatons sped off the end of the conveyor, marching into a line of other finished mechanical creatures, and then stopping and shutting down.

More than a hundred completed automatons stood in front of me, with so many more being fabricated. I gasped.

"Amazing, isn't it?" Ivan asked.

That was one word for it. I found myself getting chills and instinctively clutched Ivan's arm.

His arm was firm, and I almost pulled away the moment I realized what I'd done, but I stopped myself.

He looked down at me, amusement in his countenance. "I understand such a military apparatus must be intimidating to someone unaccustomed to such sights. However, it is the future of warfare. My men proved so unreliable in this last campaign. These will operate much more smoothly."

"How do they run?" I asked.

Ivan grinned. "Perhaps after we are wed I will show you. I can't have you running off with state secrets." He moved forward, and I allowed him to slip from my grasp.

It was a silly gesture. I didn't need his protection. These were lifeless metal creatures, not anything that would attack me. Especially with Ivan present.

He stood in front of one of the automatons, inspecting it. His face reflected in the shining metal of the completely flat machine's head. "They're elegant," Ivan said.

I assumed he was talking to himself more than to me. I didn't find anything elegant about them. The flat metal of their faces, the gears and pulleys along their joints—they looked like abominations to me.

Another figure came from around the assembly line, a woman wearing a dark dress down to her ankles, her arms covered, modestly attired—though, with her figure, it was difficult for any possible modesty. She came to us and stopped, and I noticed she had the same brilliant blue eyes as Ivan.

"Kristina," Ivan said, in a cool and formal tone.

"Brother," the woman replied, smiling. "As you can see, we're ahead of schedule for this next batch. They're about ready for military testing."

"The programming is complete, then?" Ivan asked.

"Yes." Kristina knocked her knuckles on one of the automaton's faces. It *clanged*, hollow. "Surprise."

"You should let me know of these progressions immediately. I have to adjust war plans accordingly," Ivan said.

"I didn't want to say anything until we were completely sure. I know how you don't like to be let down."

They stood facing each other for a long moment before Ivan nodded.

What was going on here? I looked between them. Ivan had a sister? I hadn't heard of this, though I knew little of his family.

Kristina sized me up, giving me a once over. "This is the Rislandian girl you've been so besotted with?"

"I am not besotted." Ivan crossed his arms.

Kristina rolled her eyes. "Interested in for *tactical* purposes." She shrugged. "Whatever makes you feel better about it. She's shorter than I expected."

"I'm taller than you," I spat back at her.

By the way she looked at me with piercing eyes—not too dissimilar from Ivan's—I wished I hadn't spoken.

"Yes, but the way Ivan speaks about you, one would have thought you were a giant." Her eyes glinted. "Anyway, I have work to do." Before I could find a way to respond, Kristina gave me a fake smile and spun to return to her factory.

Ivan shook his head. "She is infuriating. But she is one of the most detail-oriented, well-organized people I know. Men and women have different strengths, you see. I have the big picture, she completes the painting. It's why this empire runs as such a well-oiled machine."

What could I say on the matter? I didn't know her any better than I knew Ivan. But strangely, his working relationship and small rivalry with his sister humanized him.

Despite trying to appear otherwise, her light teasing clearly bothered him. He had emotions. It meant he wasn't a calculating machine like these automatons. I didn't know what to do with that information any more than I knew what to do about the automaton factory. I to had find a way to stop the fighting with Rislandia before these things could be deployed. Otherwise, Rislandia would be in for a lot of pain.

CHAPTER 12

THE STREETS OUTSIDE had descended into chaos.

Hundreds of people flooded the industrial district—pushing, screaming, yelling. They wore dark clothes and black masks, making the individuals unidentifiable. I couldn't make any sense of it. Ivan and I couldn't reach the car. The angry mob cut us off.

How had so many people assembled in so little of time without us noticing?

Men started shouting at Ivan and me. Someone threw rocks at me, hitting my thigh. It stung. I winced.

Ivan stepped in front of me, shielding me from the angry crowd. Men shouted at us. I didn't see any women present. This had to be organized—perhaps things in the Wyranth weren't as idyllic as it might seem. And Ivan didn't have any security. How could he of all people have let this happen?

Unless he had no idea it was coming. The extent of the planning of this rebellion shocked to me.

The driver broke through the crowd to reach us. He saluted Ivan. "Sir, get in the car."

Ivan moved forward. I tried to follow, but someone grabbed me by the wrist and pulled me back into the crowd.

The group shouted over each other. Anger filled their voices, but nothing they said made sense. I had no idea what was going on. Too many people pulled me in different directions.

Ivan turned, but it was too late. I drifted too far from him. I reached out a hand toward him, but more men crowded in front of me, cutting me off from him.

Just as I thought it couldn't get crazier, the warehouse factory doors burst open. Automatons marched out, making whirring noises much like the engines of an airship or some of the Wyranth's artillery. They took steps together, and then they fanned out.

Men pushed automatons down, but they kept coming from the factory. They stretched their metal arms out and used them as bludgeoning instruments, smashing into men's arms, ribs, heads. When the men fell, unlike the automatons, they didn't get back up.

Gunshots sounded. The bullets *clanged* as they ricocheted off the metal of these creatures. Someone went down in the street. Blood pooled.

"Hold your fire!" Someone shouted. "They're immune."

"There's too many of them," another man said.

The automatons cleared a path in the middle of the street as the crowds pulled me further and further away.

Ivan took a position behind the automatons, not heading for the car, but looking for me. I spotted him for a moment, and I tried to scream, but someone stuffed a cloth in my mouth to gag me. I waved frantically, but Ivan couldn't see me in the commotion. Too many people packed into the streets to make it back to the factory, and my assailants pulled me further and further away.

The automatons grabbed anything close to them, smashing the men, beating them brutally.

Tears streaked down my eyes. I turned to see who grabbed me. It was clearly a man, but in his baggy, black clothing and mask, he was indistinguishable from dozens of others around me. But why? What could they want with me?

The men who pulled me away led me around a corner, away from the fighting and the automatons. The sound of more gunshots echoed through the streets, as did the shouting and screams of pain. What had this been about? I still couldn't believe what I'd been caught in.

The man who grabbed me threw me into a horse cart and then jumped in himself. "Go!" he shouted.

A driver cracked his whip, and horses carried us away. I was trapped in a strange foreign country alone, kidnapped by these strange rioters. I wished I hadn't listened to Ivan and had brought Marina along. How could I have been so foolish? This was even worse than being in the Wyranth dungeons or the slave quarters of the Nightmen. I was helpless here, and I didn't have any hope of rescue.

I didn't have enough of my bearings to recognize where the men took me. They used side and back streets, obscured by shadows which dulled the backs of the bright houses and shops.

They paused in a dirty alley, the horses clacking their hooves to a stop. One of the men jumped off and pulled a small circle of metal from the street. It revealed a ladder and darkness below. Another man pulled me from the cart and pushed me to it. "Down," he said.

I looked down there. The stench made me wrinkle my nose. It had to be a sewage system. "I'm not going down there."

"Then I'm going to push you," the man said.

Having little choice, and no real means of escape—as the alley ended with a wall on one end, and the men blocked me from the opposite way—I descended the rungs of the ladder into the depths of the Wyranth capital.

The sewer had water running through it, or at least I thought it was water. It also contained sludge. I didn't want to get into it. The Wyranth led me along a slippery path on its edge, which made me feel like each footfall could be my last. Darkness filled the sewers, leaving only the light of a handheld gas lamp to guide us.

Something shrieked down further along the line.

"What's that?" I asked.

"Never mind," one of the men said.

My imagination got the best of me. What if it were a monster, living off of the strange sewage in the darkness? I didn't want to think of it. I'd had my fill of strange creatures.

Something scampered across my toes. I looked down to see little eyes beading in the darkness as I passed. I yelped.

One of the men pushed me forward. "Stop that. It's just some rats. Ain't gonna hurt nobody."

"Rats are filled with disease!" I said.

"Pfft," the man said. "Keep up."

We continued along the path until we took a small step up on the left, which led into a circular corridor. This didn't seem to have anything to do with the sewage system, appearing to be dug out, and without the sturdy walls the main line provided. Roots dangled from the ceiling, some hitting me in the face as I walked. I couldn't avoid them. Someone had gone to a lot of trouble to remain secret.

A metal vault door stood in front of us. A combination lock secured it. I gasped as someone shoved me toward it. One of the men turned the combination multiple times to open the lock, and when he did, it revealed an underground city of sorts, or at least a dormitory.

Gas lamps illuminated two levels of holes dug into the sides of the cavern, with stairs and a balcony surrounding. Beyond the opening in the giant room were inset rows of rusted bars. This was some ancient prison yard, long since forgotten and buried.

When we entered the large yard, people came out of the cells to get a look at us. Guards stood on the second level, pointing rifles downward. Everyone seemed on edge and careful.

A man stepped forward, muscular, hard-looking, with a scar under his right eye. "The riot commenced, Jacin?"

"As planned, Kade," my captor said.

Kade looked me over. His eyes went wide and then he grinned. "You were able to capture Zaira von Monocle?" He burst out laughing.

Jacin removed his mask, revealing a man in his thirties or forties with long scraggly hair damp with sweat. "It's hot under those masks. But yes, I was able to procure quite a bonus for us."

"I can't believe it," Kade said.

I crossed my arms, feeling as if I were being scrutinized under a magnifying glass by the way the others peered at me. I had to appear strong, though. I'd been captured before. If I showed any sign of weakness with men like this, they would take advantage.

"There is a problem I should report," Jacin said.

"What's that?"

"The Iron Emperor has amassed a whole army of those automatons. He deployed them against the riot. We had to run as quickly as we could to get out of there, but there will be a lot of bloodshed," Jacin said.

Kade crinkled his forehead. I could tell from his eyes he was a smart man, and he was in charge here. "The sacrifices of those killed will be remembered. But we have come too far to stop now. We'll have to find a way to deal with these automatons."

Jacin frowned. "They seem invincible."

"With more bloodshed, more will rise up. The Iron Emperor won't be able to suppress word of this," Kade said.

"One can only hope," Jacin said.

Kade returned his attention to me. "I'm sorry, Ms. von Monocle. We've been rude." He motioned toward one of the cells. "Would you like to join me in my office to discuss how you might be able to help us? I'm afraid we don't have much in terms of refreshments, but there's a war going on outside. Resources have to be allocated carefully." Bitterness dripped from his words.

I couldn't tell if he was sincere or sarcastic. What I could offer him? He had some gall, to drag me here and make such a proposition.

Before I could formulate any response, he turned and headed for the cell. Jacin moved along with him. They didn't seem worried I'd run. Where could I go to? They'd dragged me into the depths. I wouldn't get far.

I had no interest in helping these people. All I wanted to do was get back and help *my* people by making sure they received what we'd bargained for. I doubted Ivan would give airship technology in exchange for a missing bride-to-be. But I was unable to do anything about it now. I had to play along and listen. I lifted my skirts to step over uneven, rocky flooring, following these strange men into an ancient prison cell.

CHAPTER 13

KADE RESTED HIS elbows on the worn table, sitting on a wooden chair across from me. The furniture creaked with each movement—dirty and not very comfortable at all, but fitting for the decor of a makeshift office derived from a buried former prison.

"We've been planning for nearly a year," Kade said as if he'd rehearsed this speech several times. "When we heard Rislandians broke into our city and its prison, it gave us hope. There were only a few of us at first—Jacin, myself, and a small circle of support. We met quietly in our houses, but before long, friends told friends and we couldn't keep it contained in a residence anymore without the police noticing."

I listened and nodded. I should have been scared. After all, these people kidnapped me. But for some strange reason, I wasn't afraid. I started to understand how my father had stood strong in so many tough situations. It's what it meant to be a von Monocle.

"Our crew grew a lot faster than I would have hoped," Kade continued. "Jacin here found this place—don't ask me how—and monitored it for a month to make sure no one knew where it was or how to get here before we moved our group."

Kade motioned past the bars. Dozens of people gathered, watching us curiously.

"We moved our meetings here soon after," Jacin said.

"Meetings for what?" I asked, scanning between the gentlemen. I still wasn't sure what they wanted from me.

Kade and Jacin glanced at each other, then Kade turned his attention back to me. "I'm sorry, I figured you knew. We are the resistance to the Iron Emperor's rule. It's all very secretive for now. Today marked our first public action in causing a riot where the Iron Emperor would be. We wanted to create a scene that couldn't be ignored."

"Your presence was a bonus," Jacin said.

"You obviously know who I am," I said. It was strange to think. These people from hundreds of miles away knew my face well enough to associate a name with it. I supposed Baron von Monocle must have been infamous in the Wyranth Empire.

"Of course," Kade said. "Everyone does. You and your father have been a thorn in the Wyranth's side for decades."

"I couldn't believe I'd spotted you in that crowd. Nor that you were here..." Jacin said, narrowing his eyes. "Why are you in Wyranth with the Iron Emperor, anyway?"

This had gone from a strange kidnapping, to friendly conversation, to my being put on the spot. Should I answer them? I didn't know anything about these men, or how they'd react to finding out the truth of my being here. I also didn't have a great story as to why else I'd be here. "A diplomatic mission," I said. It wasn't a complete lie, just leaving out the details. It sounded good enough to me that I relaxed my shoulders.

They seemed to buy the story. "Ah," Kade said, disappointment filling his eyes. "Does this mean Rislandia is conceding in the fight against the Wyranth?"

"Not yet," I said. "Though it seems Iv—" I stopped myself, not sure if his name was public knowledge. "...the Iron Emperor is interested in ending the hostilities."

Jacin shook his head. "Should have never happened in the first place."

This was interesting. "What do you mean?" I asked.

"That's why we started the resistance," Kade answered for him. "Since he decided to embark upon this quest for more land, all resources have been devoted toward the military. Foodstuffs go to the army first, workers are on rations. Sometimes we're even ordered to house soldiers. It's been torture. People are starving. It's miserable, and we're all asked to work extra shifts to keep it going. Now... we're being replaced with these automatons. The Iron Emperor has no concern for his people, only his strange schemes."

When Ivan and I had talked prior, he had always told me the land he meant to take from Rislandia was to get the Wyranth *more* resources. This story didn't make sense with what he'd told me, and I didn't think Ivan was a liar on this point, but I could see him losing perspective of the common folk in his singular focus.

Still, a resistance was a big matter to discover. We hadn't heard of anything of the sort in Rislandia. We would want to support them if we could. At least, we would have up until recently. Now Ivan wanted to stop the fighting, or at least so he said. We couldn't support an uprising on this side of the border in the midst of such negotiations, could we?

Kade smiled. "I see you understand, and you're considering helping us. Our own resources are meager. The people here scrape together what they can, but it's as I said, everything has been going toward the war effort as of late. It's hard to get aether fuel for the lamps to keep this hideaway lit."

"I know the feeling," I said, recalling how the dim lights of Rislandia City when I'd walked through her streets last.

The conversation paused. The men wanted to ask me something and had been working toward it. Kade finally broke the silence. "Do you think it will be possible for you to send word of us to Rislandia, and see if you could get us some help, supplies, anything?" His eyes shone brightly at me with hope.

What could I tell him? We were just as strapped for resources. We didn't have the ability to do anything on this side of the border. I couldn't promise anything, but this was what leadership and diplomacy was. "I'll do my best," I said. It wasn't a commitment to do anything other than tell King Malaky about what was going on here. I could handle that.

"I'm sure you have great sway over your kingdom. Anything could be helpful," Jacin said.

"Is there anything I can bring back? Information you have, perhaps?" I asked. This would be the real test.

"The automatons," Kade said. "There's a lot more of them than you see. I've heard rumblings thousands are being created on the Isle du Mystere in the south, enough to overwhelm all of Rislandia."

That news sent a shiver down my spine. What chance did we have against a full army of mindless automatons,? "Do you know how to stop them?" I asked.

Kade shook his head. "Not yet. But we'll get that information. You get us supplies. Food, bullets, guns, and we'll find their weakness."

It sounded like a great trade, and just what our people needed. But I was here, in the Wyranth Empire, stuck for the foreseeable future. They didn't know that, of course. My heart sank at the deception, but if they knew the truth, would they even let me out of here? I doubted it. At that point, I'd be used as a hostage, or worse, I'd be killed.

Could I go back on my promise to marry Ivan? We wouldn't get the airship technology, but now we had some informants within the Wyranth Empire. I bit down on my lip as I considered. It would be a riskier proposition than trusting Ivan for the airship plans. If he truly did have a giant army of automatons ready to take on Rislandia, we couldn't merely hope to find a way to stop them.

It was something I'd have to think about later. I could consult with Marina on it when I got back to the palace. For now, I had to keep these Resistance men's respective trusts and get out of here.

"I need to get back," I said, realizing they hadn't made me any promises about how long I would be held captive here. "My kidnapping is bound to cause an uproar and might put more of your people in danger."

Kade nodded. "You're right. I'm glad we had this opportunity to talk. Hopefully, when this all shakes out, we can have a friendly relationship between our two countries."

He presumed a lot and clearly thought further into the future than I did. All I wanted to do was to make sure Rislandia survived these next few months, and then I'd figure out something from there. I couldn't predict who would be leading the Wyranth Empire by then, but I doubted these people had the means to truly take on Ivan if they were coming to me for help.

It was a wide-eyed naiveté I might have had before the invasion, but I understood the limitations of the real world. At the same time, I knew better than to voice any negative opinions of what they were doing. They may have acted friendly to me so far, but if they had an inclination I might not be able to do as much for them as they thought, their hospitality could turn quickly.

"Jacin, can you show her out?" Kade asked.

"Of course," Jacin said, motioning to the cell entrance. "We'll get you set somewhere above ground, close to the palace. You'll have to make it back from there."

"I'm sure I can handle it," I said, hoping it would be true.

CHAPTER 14

WHEN WE ROSE from the sewer system again, the sun had already set. Lights shone on the main streets, but we entered the city in the darkness of an alley. Jacin stayed on the ladder which led below, looking up at me as I stood and smoothed my skirts.

"This is where I depart," Jacin said.

"Where's the palace?" I said, spinning and trying to orient myself. It didn't do me much good, as I didn't know my way around the Wyranth capital.

"Two blocks to the right. You won't be able to miss it once you get into the street. It has a giant light which shines upward, a beacon for the rest of the city," Jacin said.

I supposed I couldn't expect him to escort me into an area where we'd be seen, though the foreign city made my spine creep, being alone here. I couldn't believe I wanted to rely on my kidnapper to keep me safe, but I felt more secure around him and his people than I did amongst the general Wyranth population. "I hope we can meet again soon," I said.

"Me as well. Good luck to you, Baron von Monocle." He slipped the cover back over his head and disappeared.

I was alone.

What was I going to tell Ivan about where I'd been? Even if I told him the complete truth, he would find it suspicious. I'd met with his rebels. They had been kind to me and let me go. Surely, he'd think I was hiding something.

I had no idea what I would say.

A cool breeze highlighted the spring air, crisp but not burdensomely so. I jogged down the alley until I came into the light.

Only a few carts and carriages traveled through the streets, with even fewer gentlemen walking the street in front of me. The Wyranth were strict—it wouldn't surprise me if they had a curfew.

I slowed my pace as I spotted the palace, which had lights shining on its walls just as Jacin had told me. Automatons loomed over my walk, staring at me as I moved toward my destination.

What if those things malfunctioned and attacked people? There had to be some way to disable them. I wouldn't trust machines on my streets like this, but Ivan had said they were more reliable than their human counterparts.

Ivan's personal guard and servants spotted me before I reached the palace and escorted me inside. They hurried me along, acting like their lives depended upon my safety. No one had bothered me outside, but everyone was in such a tense mood. One would have thought Rislandians were invading the city.

The guards brought me into Ivan's study, telling me to wait for him. Despite my best efforts in the sewer, I must have been covered in dirt and other things I didn't want to think about. I couldn't smell anything about myself, but by the way the servants kept their noses away from me, I'm sure my fragrance wasn't the most elegant.

Ivan rushed into the study. He shut the doors behind him, trapping me alone with him. His eyes had a fire in them I hadn't seen before. "What happened to you? Why do you smell like that?"

"I... got lost," I said. It was a thin story, but the best I could do. "There were so many people. I didn't know what to do."

"My people were searching for you everywhere. You couldn't have been out on the streets of the city," Ivan said. He was interrogating me harder than when he had me as a prisoner.

I stuck to my story. "I was frightened. A man took me inside and offered me tea. I didn't want to come back out until I was sure it was safe." Ivan's eyes still bored into me. I needed to turn the conversation elsewhere. "What happened out there? Do you have riots often?"

"No," Ivan said. "Never. Thankfully, I had my automatons to handle the situation. Otherwise I might have been assassinated." He narrowed his eyes. "We captured a couple of the rabble-rousers. My men are interrogating them now."

Ivan paced to his bookshelf, standing in front of it and scanning the titles. I watched him but said nothing.

"You met with the resistance leaders, didn't you?" Ivan asked.

"I don't know what you're talking about," I said.

Ivan turned around. "Don't lie to me. You're not good at it." He had his fist balled.

Was he going to hit me? Was this what I would be in for when I married him?

He must have spotted me recoiling as he let his hand go slack. "I apologize," Ivan said. "I shouldn't be angry at you. You didn't start this, and of course, if I were a resistance leader and I had word of you in the city, I would have orchestrated this very scenario." He rapped his fingers on his pant leg. "Yes, that's exactly what I would have done. Who was the leak who let them know we were going to tour the factory is the question I should be asking."

Ivan stepped toward me again. He grabbed me by the arm. "Zaira, you have to tell me where their base of operations is," he said.

"I can't, they led me away from their place like we were in a maze. It was dark and I couldn't see anything," I said quietly.

His grip tightened on me. "This isn't a joke. This is a matter of my country's survival, and you might not realize it, but you are in as much danger as I am if this society breaks down. We have to nip this in the bud."

I tried to pull back, but he wouldn't let me free. "You're hurting me," I said.

Ivan released me, and then let out a deep breath. "I just apologized for my anger, didn't I? I need to learn to maintain calm. There's no benefit to being angry. It clouds strategy." His eyes searched me.

I still didn't know what I should say. I looked him in the eyes. They were beautiful, deep as they'd always been. Despite his rage, I found myself more sympathetic toward him. He didn't want to hurt me and chastised himself for making me uncomfortable. It was still so odd, but he cared about me. "Ivan?"

"Yes?"

"Why are you so insistent upon marrying me? None of this makes any sense."

The room fell into silence. Ivan stared at his books for a long time. He'd been so evasive about this question, but I needed to know the answer. Couldn't he see that?

Finally, Ivan sighed. "I suppose now is as good a time as any to tell you." He spun on his heel, motioning to the couch. "Have a seat."

I sat down, unbunching my skirts as best as I could.

Ivan helped himself to a seat next to me. It startled me at first. Usually, he sat across from me, but this was an intensely personal matter to discuss. His eyes focused hard on me, reading into my soul. It wasn't quite like the way Ethan did, where he seemed eager for me, but a more calculating manner.

"Where should I begin that won't make this sound crazy?" Ivan chuckled to himself. "As you're aware, I'm quite studied in world history. Historical battles fascinate me to a great degree, but there's such a beautiful tapestry woven within this world. It leaves me no doubt that a divine artist sculpted our existence, but I digress."

I'd never thought of how we were created as people. The words made me uncomfortable, just like his close presence. I found myself leaning back into the corner of the couch, trapped by its dimensions. I wanted to run, but where would I go?

"This has to do with your airship, the reason it won't fly, and the reason it flew before," Ivan said.

"How?" He confused me even more.

"This may take several discussions," Ivan said. Whether he was stalling, or truly trying to figure out how to explain the information to me, I couldn't tell. "Are you familiar with any myths and legends from thousands of years ago?"

I sucked in my bottom lip, considering. "My mother used to read me a story about the giants crossing the Golgmarsh Ocean. I also read a fairy tale about elves..."

Ivan put a hand up. "I'll stop you there. We all know elves aren't real, but we've both come into contact with the evolutionary descendants of what used to be giants. My scientists were able to revert some of the degeneration that's turned them into telepathic blobs."

"I'm aware," I said, trying not to let my anger seethe. Because of his scientists' work, I'd lost my airship.

"Ah, right," Ivan said, acknowledging my mood. He didn't have remorse over what he'd done. "I've had archaeologists and historians research the matter. Giants were once very real, nearly human like you and I, but larger obviously. They originated on the Zenwey continent, then propagated. Many of the original giants didn't have lifespans like us, however. Those are the ones we found burrowed and degenerated in our lands. But there was some... interspecies breeding that occurred."

"I've heard about that," I said, recalling my adventure over to the foreign continent. "There are these blue-skinned feral people in Zenwey called the Nightmen. Their legends say they were descended from a giant and a human princess who ran away together."

"Really?" Ivan raised a brow. "Fascinating. I'll have to have you detail your experience to my chief archaeologist. But that does fit with what we know."

Footsteps sounded on the tile outside the room. Someone jiggled the handle to the door.

"This is a private meeting," Ivan said for the benefit of the newcomer.

The door opened anyway. "Really, Ivan?" asked a female voice. In came Kristina, her expression all smiles. "Are you making untoward advances on our poor guest?"

"Hardly," Ivan said, his expression going flat. "Now isn't a good time for your teasing."

Kristina placed a hand on her chest. "I merely wished to see how you and your guest were doing after the awful peasant revolt." She glanced between us. "What *did* I walk in on?"

"We're fine, Kristina," Ivan said in a warning tone. "Can we talk later?"

Her eyes widened, and her smile broadened. She moved over to the chair across from us and plopped down on it. "You're telling her the real reason you brought her here, aren't you? Oh, this is good. Has he talked about the magical crystals he believes hold the world together yet?" Her eyes glimmered with mockery.

"Crystals?" I blinked.

Ivan sighed. "There'll be much to discuss later. But no, we were getting to the history of the giants."

"Ahh," Kristina said, rubbing her hands together. "That part, at least, is well-substantiated. How much do you know of the creatures?"

"Enough to know I don't like them," I said.

Kristina laughed.

"You're not helping," Ivan warned.

"Okay, I'll be quiet. Continue your conversation," Kristina said.

"Where were we before we were so rudely interrupted?" Ivan asked, and then snapped his fingers. "Giants, right. When our scientists first ran experiments for our soldier serums, we discovered a small minority of people had stronger reactions than the others. Some soldiers get stronger, more aggressive, more focused, but this group seemed connected with the creature living in the heart of Devil's Mountain. They could sense its hunger, its anger, its fears."

I recalled when I'd been given some of the serum to help repair my wounds. When my people then set the bomb in Devil's Mountain, I went into a strange fit. It was like I'd lost control of my senses. I had been filled with rage, and then strange visions. "This happened to me," I said under my breath.

Ivan grinned. "That's right. You took the serum."

"Only a small amount, and only once, not enough to be affected by the withdrawals," I said.

"It still confirms my research," Ivan said. He turned to Kristina. "Do you see? I was right."

Kristina had a look of amusement on her face. "Uh-huh."

Ivan took my hand. It was such a sudden move I gasped. Everything became awkward all at once, both sets of those beautiful, imperial eyes locked on me.

Ivan didn't back away after my outburst but maintained his grip. "Zaira," he said. "Your lineage descends from the giants. The blood has been diluted over generations, but you have their genetics, the abilities that come with it."

"Abilities?" I asked. This was all so absurd. How could I be descended from giants? I was a little taller than average height for a Rislandian woman, but not by much.

"Have you noticed anything?" Ivan pressed.

I considered. Nothing seemed out of the ordinary. In fact, I'd been downright clumsy in my first days of adventuring. I'd gotten better, but I still was nowhere near as dexterous as someone like Talyen. What could he mean?

Then, it struck me.

"The von Monocle luck," I whispered.

"What do you mean?" Ivan asked.

"I seem to have an uncanny ability to survive certain situations which would typically mean overwhelming odds against my survival. It's a running joke in Rislandia, or at least a running myth. It comes from my father."

Ivan shook his head. "No, Zaira. That's not the lineage I researched. Your giant's blood comes from your mother's side."

CHAPTER 15

"SOUNDS LIKE YOU had a crazy day," Marina said, sitting cross-legged on the end of the bed in my guest quarters.

I paced the room, stopping in front of the mirror to get a view of Marina behind me. "I did. But I still don't understand."

"What don't you understand?" Marina asked. She was so patient. She listened to me. Her friendship was invaluable.

"What he wants from it. He said we would talk about it another time. Everything's such a strange machination with him. It's frustrating," I said.

Marina tilted her head to get a better look at me. "You like him," she said.

"I do not."

"Do too."

"Do not."

"Do too."

I turned around to face her. "He's interesting, I'll give you that. But I am fully committed to Ethan. At least I was." I shook my head to try to clear it. "I don't know. It's not an option now. I have to fulfill my obligation to help Rislandia, right?"

"You'll do what you feel you have to," Marina said. The way she watched me let me know she was skeptical.

"I wish you wouldn't look at me like that," I said.

"Like what?"

I let out a deep sigh, moving toward the bed and letting myself fall back on the clear area. My head hit the pillows. "All of this is so confusing. It's like a whirlwind has upended my life, and I have no idea what's going on."

"Now you understand how everyone else feels around you," Marina said.

"I'm serious," I said.

"So am I."

I stared at the ceiling. If Ivan was right, I had *giant* blood flowing through me, informing my actions...a part of my person. It made sense the way he described it, given what I'd experienced when I'd come across giants in the past. I could almost believe I had a kinship with them if it weren't so fantastical a concept.

"What are you going to do about it?" Marina asked.

"I don't know," I said. The words came out more of a pout than I'd intended, but I was so frustrated I wanted to pull my hair out. "I still need to figure out why the giant blood is so important to him. It's a lot to process."

"I'm sure you'll figure it out," Marina said. "I was worried about you, you know. I thought about snapping the Iron Emperor's neck if you didn't make it back."

Marina cared about me. As much as violence colored her words, she meant to communicate her loyalty. And it meant a lot to me. I sat up. "Funny part is, I wasn't all that scared. Do you know what happened?"

"Only bits and pieces," Marina said.

I kept my voice low, and a hand over my mouth, in case someone listened through the walls. I told her about the riots, about the Resistance, and how they'd taken me away to recruit Rislandian assistance for their movement.

Marina looked at me and pointed to her ears—a reminder that Ivan probably had spies listening in on our every word.

I hadn't said anything I wouldn't have otherwise, but it was still good to remember. We were in hostile enemy territory, no matter how accommodating the Wyranth had been to us so far. If Ivan didn't need something from me, he would slit my throat.

And it was good I hadn't gone further into the story of the giants. Marina had her own symptoms dealing with the giant, though not the same mental connection I did. Her reaction had been one of violence. Perhaps this was the reaction of someone who didn't have the giant's blood? It was something Rislandian scientists would have to analyze.

"What about the airship plans?" I asked, trying to change the subject. "You were going to inspect those today?"

"I did. From your description of the journals you had, they seem authentic. There's full plans there, though I can't make heads or tails of the mathematical equations on them."

My heart sank. I had hoped Ivan was bluffing. That I'd be able to leave here, to not follow through with my end of the bargain and call him a liar and a fraud. All of my hope vanished with Marina's words.

"I don't know what to do," I said, searching Marina for answers. She was so cool and collected in these situations.

Marina scrunched her nose and pursed her lips. "I'm not so sure either. It depends on what's most important to you."

"Rislandia," I said without equivocation.

"Then I suggest you keep discovering what you can. The Iron Emperor wants to trust you with a lot of his ideas. You're in the best position to find out his grand plans and make sure they don't hurt the people back home."

I nodded. It was a lot of responsibility. This wasn't as simple as going out on an airship, adventuring, or ordering the cannoneers to fire all guns. I had to be patient, a quality I didn't often exhibit.

Ivan wanted me for my genetics, my bloodline. He thought it was important for some reason. Could it be he wanted me to adventure and detect more buried giants for use in creating his serums? I could hardly believe he'd be so foolish as to try that again, given how feral his soldiers became when they took it. Besides, Ivan moved onto creating these automatons to replace his men in such work. There had to be more to it.

"I'll do my best," I said, resolved. I reached into the small pouch I had strapped around my waist and set the micro-camera on her leg. It had film containing the automatons on there. At least I'd done something. "You should head back to Rislandia, though. Let King Malaky know what's going on and that the airship plans are authentic. They'll want to know. Maybe we can do some good in the meantime while I figure out what this crazy emperor is up to?"

"Aye aye, Baronette," Marina said, clutching the micro-camera. It felt almost like old times again when she'd said that.

I looked to the window. How I longed to be up in the sky instead of trapped dirtside in this palace.

CHAPTER 16

SERVANTS SUMMONED ME to breakfast the next morning.

I ate with Kristina, who I learned didn't live in the palace, but lingered around because of interest in Ivan's relationship with me. She appeared far too amused by the whole situation. I wanted to ask her why, but I also had the sneaking suspicion she might say something blunt about my person which I didn't want to hear. Consequently, I ate my breakfast in relative silence, exchanging pleasantries and small talk as needed.

Marina packed her belongings and readied to depart soon after we ate. She gave me a hug, pausing to speak in my ear, "Are you sure you'll be okay here alone?"

I pulled back, smiling to reassure her, though the truth of the matter was the prospect of my being stuck here chilled me to my core. "It's nothing I haven't done before. At least the accommodations are better this time."

Marina snorted. "You're hilarious, Baronette."

I shrugged. "Safe travels," I said.

"For steam and country," Marina said, saluting. She turned and headed off to a driver and his horseless carriage.

Ivan had given permission for Marina to return to Rislandia. She would then be allowed back to assist me, assuming Ivan told the truth. We had to hope he held sincerity in allowing her to depart with information for our kingdom, though so far, he hadn't pulled any tricks on us. How long would his goodwill last?

"Excuse me, ma'am," a servant said to me after I'd watched Marina drive away.

I turned to the servant. "Yes?"

"The Iron Emperor would like you to join him in his Devil's Mountain laboratory," he said.

Kristina came slinking up to my side. "I bet he would."

Her presence made me want to shrink inside myself, though I couldn't explain why. I glanced at her. "I thought we destroyed the facility inside the mountain."

"That was a year ago," she said. "A lot has changed. You'll see. I've been waiting for him to show you this. It's been his obsession since he discovered it."

"What's *it*?" I asked, getting annoyed with her obtuse manner of speaking.

"I'm not going to be the one to reveal his surprises," Kristina said. She motioned the servant ahead and moved ahead with a small skip in her step. She enjoyed torturing me far too much.

I could do nothing but follow, and we soon found our way into the familiar dungeon below the palace, where I'd been held a year prior. It was as dark and dingy as before, gas lamps periodically lighting the stone walls and floors. Someone wailed in the background, making me shiver. Neither the servant nor Kristina took any special note of the sound.

We wound our way through the maze of corridors until the stone subsided into an area dug out of dirt. The last time I'd been here, my father and knights led us into the Wyranth's serum production facility inside Devil's Mountain. It's where we first discovered the existence of giants, the glowing blue gelatinous blobs that supplied the Wyranth with their blood. What would I discover this time?

We passed a storeroom with crates piled high, before the pathway opened into the large facility. Several platforms adorned the open area. A lot of machinery lingered around a small tunnel on the other side that led outside and to the opposite side of Devil's Mountain.

Instead of soldiers, automatons stood guard, lifeless and unmoving, but their blank faces stared at me. Several scientists in lab coats moved about, manning machines, taking notes, conversing amongst themselves.

Other workers labored in constructing machinery. One worker cranked a machine which lit a large torch, the flames of which were used to melt and forge metal. My eyes widened. The torch could be used as a weapon just as easily as a device to construct something.

Kristina led me to a big machine up against the railing of the pit where the giant used to be. The pit was cleared now, empty. Ivan stood by it, talking with one of his scientists.

He looked up as we approached, his swimming blue eyes focusing on me. "Ah, good, Zaira. You're here." His gaze found Kristina. "Sister," he said flatly.

"Good morning to you too, dear brother," Kristina said. "Is today the day?"

I thought about what Kristina was going to ask. Was Ivan going to present me with a ring? He'd still yet to formally propose to me, though I supposed he didn't have to. All had been arranged and anything we did would be superfluous.

But Ivan thrived on formalities and traditions. I could see him mining this mountain to find some precious ore where his laborers would forge the ring for me.

Why was I fantasizing about this? I had to snap out of it. There were too many questions, and I craved answers.

Ivan ignored Kristina and took me by the hand, bringing me over to the strange machine. It had two inset areas, with wires protruding from them, which had small pads on their ends.

"What did she mean by 'is today the day'?" I asked.

"I told you there was a lot to discuss. Part of the matter was the giant blood of your lineage, but there's another component."

He dropped my hand. "When we appropriated the plans for your airship, my scientists combed through them. What we found was astounding and verifies hundreds of myths and legends from antiquity. You see, the airship *Liliana* should never have been able to fly. Its bulky mass would take too much energy to lift off of the ground. It's a physical impossibility."

"So I've heard," I said, recalling my meeting with Harkerpal and his teams of engineers.

"When there's a physical impossibility, there are two options. One, to scrap the idea entirely, which didn't occur, or two, find some way to bend reality to your will. Your people may understand a lot about the airship, but there was one element left out of your current redesign."

I looked at him in disbelief. "Harkerpal knew that ship like the back of his hand."

"Of what he was told," Ivan said. "He wasn't the one who originally designed the engine."

I placed my hands on my hips. "I'll give. What did he miss?"

"I'm going to show you, as you will probably have the same reaction my sister did if I simply explain the matter," Ivan said.

Kristina huffed.

"Dr. Metzengerstein, can you please start the device?"

A man in a lab coat and goggles stepped between us, turning knobs and devices until the machine in front of us whirred. Steam shot out the cracks in the center ahead of us, and a platform raised, mechanically clicking as gears turned. It lifted to reveal a rock inside, about the length of my palm, but the width of two of my fingers. There didn't seem to be anything special about it, but two pieces of metal jammed against it, creating a circuit.

I'd heard the name Dr. Metzengerstein several times in briefing reports. He was supposedly a mad inventor much like our own Dr. von Breech, who created most of Rislandia's new technology. I had no doubt he was responsible for the automatons standing guard over us now. He had bushy eyebrows, a thicker frame but not fat, and stood a hair taller than me. He had an intense focus about him, lost in his scientific work as if the other humans in the room weren't there.

"It's ready," Dr. Metzengerstein said.

Ivan placed his hands in one of the small compartments and placed the pads on his fingers. "Zaira, if you would please join me in attaching the electrodes to your fingertips."

"What's going to happen?" I asked.

"Trust me," Ivan said. "You won't get hurt."

I did as he said. The electrodes had a sticky substance which allowed them to stay on my hands when I placed them in the small compartment. They tingled like a static shock from clothing, but less intense and never stopping. "This feels strange," I said.

"It's electricity," Dr. Metzengerstein said. "Surging from your body, feeding into the machine and back out again."

Something pulsed through the machine. It vibrated violently, wailing in protest. The rock inside the compartment rattled and glowed. But more, the cave around us shook as well, pebbles and debris dropping from above. The walls of the pit started to cave.

Ivan's eyes went wide at the scene. So much destructive power. He must have been thrilled with this.

I was horrified as the sides to the pit collapsed. Dust plumed in the cavern. I coughed after inhaling some of it. I'd had enough. I ripped my hands away, detaching the electrodes in the process.

The machine died almost instantly. The connection to me had been what powered it in its completeness.

Ivan turned to me. "Why did you stop? I wanted to see what this was capable of."

I coughed a few more times, using the sleeve of my blouse so I wouldn't cough on anyone. My eyes itched from the dust around us. Dr. Metzengerstein manned the controls of the device, ignoring us as if we weren't there at all.

How did the connection to me cause the machine to create such force? I didn't understand. The sheer amount of power it displayed frightened me to my core. This all felt so wrong, like I'd unlocked something very dark. It was almost a spiritual experience.

"I want no part of this," I said. "You said this had to do with my airship, but I have no idea what you're talking about. An airship doesn't cause earthquakes. This felt more like what the giants did."

"Because it is. Believe me, it all relates," Ivan said. "I—"

A Wyranth soldier rushed toward us and saluted Ivan. "Emperor, sir."

"Yes, Lieutenant?" Ivan said, lips curling in annoyance at the interruption.

"I've received word back from the line. The automatons did their job. The Rislandians were caught completely unprepared. The battle test was a success." The soldier's eyes brightened.

"Very good, Lieutenant. We'll proceed with phase two. This is great news," Ivan said. He turned back to me, as the Lieutenant saluted and took the turn as a dismissal.

The Rislandians had been attacked by automatons? While I slept here?

Rage filled me, a heat rising from my toes all the way to my head. My body became a teapot, ready to boil over. Ivan had made me assurances that the hostilities were going to wind down. Had this been yet another distraction to take me away from where I was needed most? The whole situation tried my patience to an extreme. Strange tests of destructive weapons, an army of machine men... This was not dialing down a war at all, it was preparing for a complete onslaught. Enough was enough.

Ivan opened his mouth to speak again. I clenched my fist, wound my arm back and socked him right in the jaw.

CHAPTER 17

THE FEW HUMAN soldiers in the room came forward to grab me, but Ivan held up a hand to stop them. "Stand down," he said.

He brought his hand to his jaw, stroking it. "You hit harder than I expected."

I wanted to hit him again, but I stood there glaring at him, defiant.

"I understand you're upset," Ivan said.

"You promised you would be bringing an end to hostilities," I said.

"That's not exactly what I promised. I only promised the airship technology, but nonetheless, this action was a defensive measure, not an aggressive one. The Rislandians were advancing upon our position in Loveridge. We were not trying to take ground."

I didn't much care about his explanation. "You sent your machines against people. Rislandians died."

"We're at war," Ivan said.

An awkward silence hung between us.

He was right, of course. If the situations were reversed, Rislandia would have sent their automatons against a Wyranth army. Casualties were a part of war, but I hated it. I thought about losing friends and family to machines, helpless to do anything against them. I crossed my arms over my chest. "If we're going to continue with this engagement, I want you to put a stop to this."

Kristina brushed her fingers against the machine behind us, casually acting as if she were paying no attention.

Ivan glowered at her. "Can you not hover?"

Kristina blinked. "Hmm?"

"You know what you're doing," Ivan said.

Kristina sighed. "Fine, I'll leave you two be. I have to get back to the factory and make sure the automatons are all ready for phase two anyway." She emphasized the end of her statement, enjoying infuriating Ivan.

"What's phase two?" I asked as Kristina walked away.

"Securing the entirety of our new holdings," Ivan said.

More automatons against our army. I couldn't allow that to continue. "You have to put a stop to it," I said.

"I'm afraid that's impossible," Ivan said.

"It's not. You can take a carriage out to the line and tell them to stand down."

"I could easily send a missive to that regard. But will the Rislandians honor a ceasefire?" Ivan asked.

"Probably not, but if we go together, it might work," I said, trying to come up with a plan. "We'll send a message across the line and make sure there's no fighting... at least until we can figure something out."

Ivan grimaced. He didn't like the idea, but I wasn't about to let up. His eyes met mine, calculating as they always did. "Very well," he said.

I opened my mouth to argue, expecting him to fight the idea further. Had he just agreed with me? My mouth hung open longer than I intended and I snapped it shut. Had I just altered the course of the war with my plea? I wondered if anyone ever spoke to Ivan like this. "Okay," I said, much more meekly.

"I suppose we should make plans," Ivan said, glancing back at his machine.

Dr. Metzengerstein made adjustments to the device with several different tools. I still had no idea what had transpired with it. "I'm confused by this whole thing. What is that rock in the middle of the machine? Why do you need me?"

Ivan clasped his hands together in front of him. "The artifact the machine uses is a crystal. Legends have it that the world was formed and the creator injected full power of reality into the crystals. I've been researching them since I came across the myths in my library. This one, I discovered when we reclaimed the wreckage after your people detonated the bomb within the mountain."

"The crystal is a power conduit?" I asked.

"In a sense. The crystals have different properties, from what I've been able to determine. The people of legends used them to enact their will on our world. Fairy tales called it magic, but these have distinctive properties that can be used scientifically. What you just experienced was your psychic energy interacting with an earth crystal."

It sounded silly, like a fairy tale, but I had to believe my eyes. "But I needed wires and a machine to use it."

"You did," Ivan said. "It's my belief that the ancients were able to manipulate these crystals with their sheer willpower. Their physiology had something to do with it, which is why I was looking for a descendant with adequate genetic material."

My forehead scrunched as I thought about it. "You interacted with it as well."

Ivan smiled at me. "I too have the giant's blood lineage. This isn't a new discovery. My father pursued your mother to great lengths to try to keep the line pure."

I hadn't known about this, though I recalled when I was in the palace the first time, Ivan mentioned my mother as if he were intimately familiar with her. Now it started to make more sense. But it was a wild fantasy. Giant blood? Magical crystals? This was his entire obsession with my family? If I hadn't seen the machine, felt the power coursing through my body, I would have thought he was crazy. I understood why Kristina acted the way she did. She must have thought her brother delusional.

Kristina. That raised a question. "Why wouldn't you use Kristina for your experiments? Doesn't she have the same blood?"

"She has a different mother," Ivan said.

I nodded. It made sense as to why they were such different creatures. "You said this had something to do with the airship..." I said, working out how all of this tied together.

Ivan watched me, but said nothing.

My eyes widened. "The *Liliana* had a crystal in its engine, didn't it? And when Harkerpal fabricated a new one, he didn't have the proper component."

"You've figured it out," Ivan said. "I knew you were intelligent."

I could return to Rislandia with this knowledge, but would anyone believe me? How could I announce there was some strange crystal that powered the airship?

No, it wouldn't work. I only had limited knowledge. I had to find out more. I glanced at Ivan again. He would keep the details secret in order to keep ahold of me. I had enough information to whet my appetite, but I was still trapped here with him. He wouldn't let me go that easily. "And you know where to get this crystal that powers the airship, don't you?"

"I do," Ivan said. "But before we can explore, we'll head to Loveridge in two days in order to stop the battle. That's more important to you, isn't it?"

CHAPTER 18

TWO DAYS LATER, Ivan ordered his guard to bring a carriage for us to travel north.

My mind reeled. Coming to the Wyranth Empire had flipped my whole world upside down in so many ways. The automatons scared me, but so did this strange crystal energy. Part of me wanted to deny any semblance of powerful crystals which could bend our reality, but I'd seen it firsthand. I'd been a part of its radiance.

I glanced at my hands. Had something within me created that shaking in the cavern?

The carriage slowed as we left the main gates of the city. Automatons stood guard, with more following after us on foot. They padded as quickly as the motor could take us along the bumpy roads outside of the Wyranth capital. Their speed irked me even more. If Ivan could create thousands of these, how would Rislandia survive?

Ivan didn't seem concerned. He had a stoic countenance as he kept his gaze forward on the road. The red mark where I'd hit him detracted from his hard visage, however.

We drove down the road in silence, and finally, I got the nerve to speak. "What are you thinking about?" I asked.

"That was the first test of the earth crystal where it worked. I'd known I needed a secondary source based on the texts I read, and that it had to be a female source, but I almost stopped believing in the old tales."

"Now you have proof," I said.

Ivan nodded. "It will quiet Kristina, at the very least. But it means I should be redoubling expeditions to find these crystals. Legends have shown them cropping up all over the world."

I perked. "An airship would be helpful in that regard."

Ivan raised a curious brow. "It would. Though I doubt Rislandia would send theirs on a mission for my sake—if they managed to get it running. Of course, we could simply conquer Rislandia."

I narrowed my eyes. "Ivan…"

He laughed. "I'm kidding."

Was he though? He didn't sound like it. I wanted to sock him in the jaw again.

We drove through the countryside. It was beautiful in the south of Wyranth during the day, with the rolling hills, sparse trees, and small settlements in the distance. The city loomed behind us, smoke rising from it from the industry, blocked by Devil's Mountain. It didn't have a giant spire and felt a lot less like home because of it. I missed the sight of my home city.

The spire! It reminded me. "Wait, we have a *Crystal* Spire in Rislandia."

"That you do. I had hoped to have time to study it further when we captured it," Ivan said. "But alas, you didn't allow us sufficient time to take root."

"The name can't be a coincidence," I said.

"Do you know the legends of the spire?"

"Just that the original settlers built it when they first came to Rislandia. A watchtower to gaze out upon the whole of the land. Though, even from the heights, I don't think one can see that far, even with the aid of a telescope."

"You can with the aid of air crystals," Ivan said.

I returned my gaze to him. "You've studied this a lot."

Ivan nodded. "The original settlers were said to be wizards, fleeing from a vast empire that covered most of the Areth continent. They had powers of various crystals the Great Areth Emperor wished to have for his mage knights. In theory they were able to activate the crystals without the use of electrodes. It's an art lost to me. Perhaps the genetics were much more closely tied to the crystals..." Ivan sighed and put his elbow up on the side of the carriage. "We'll never know. We do know they were able to build the Spire and the walls of Rislandia without the machinery we have today. All was lost in the great continental war that caused the settlers to flee again, where the settlers disappeared. Eventually, the land was resettled, and the empire splintered over the centuries. I wish I had more information."

"Me as well," I said. What I wanted to find was the crystals that could help the airship fly. Ivan had to have a way to hunt them down. I knew so little about them. Perhaps he would open up about it if I stayed with him more.

The ride lasted too many hours with my mind whirling, but I'd been on this road before, so I knew what to expect. We traveled up through the marshlands, toward the border river where the forests thickened, obscuring the view. Along the way, we stopped at several checkpoints of Wyranth soldiers who, upon seeing Ivan in the flesh, became nervous around us.

It must be nice to have that much power over everyone. But was it better to be feared? Back home, most of us loved King Malaky. I wished Ivan could see the merits of being kinder to people. But he was so singularly focused. I started to understand his quest, though it would look crazy to someone who didn't know the details. Perhaps he had to rule with an iron fist to maintain order under those conditions.

We crossed a makeshift bridge that stretched across the Border River. The carriage bounced and jolted me from side to side as we traversed it. I clutched the side of the carriage in fear the rickety bridge would break, but we managed to make it over without incident. One of the automaton's foot got stuck in a bridge plank. When it freed itself, it fell into the water. Ivan ordered our driver not to stop for it. I felt bad for the poor thing, even though I knew it was just a machine.

It took another two hours of driving before we arrived in Loveridge, and it was dark by the time we arrived. Wyranth had patrols dressed in their military uniforms with pointed helmets, and they had automatons as backup. No Rislandian citizens walked the streets. Either they had fled in fear, or they stayed inside because of the nearby battles.

Either way, the town gave me an eerie feeling. A chill made me shiver, and I wished I had a coat.

The sound of repeated gunfire blasted in the forest ahead of us. I turned my head to try to see past the log buildings of Loveridge, but even if it were daytime, I wouldn't have been able to see anything. The battle continued into the night? I supposed the automatons didn't tire. It must have been frightening for the Rislandians on the front lines.

"We have to stop the fighting," I said.

Ivan frowned. "It's dark out. We could get killed by mistake if we run to the line now."

The carriage stopped, the men in the front getting out to open the door for me. They escorted me around to where Ivan stood, stretching his legs and arms.

"It would be best to spend the evening in the local inn and see what we can do in the morning. We can then send an emissary in the hopes of parley, and get the Rislandians to stop fighting."

I shook my head. "No. You call your machines off, make them stop firing. I'll go out and try to talk to the Rislandians." I didn't wait for him to respond. He would have only told me I was foolish, but I couldn't allow more of my people to die. I hiked up my skirts, continuing down the streets.

"Zaira!" Ivan called after me. I half expected him to give chase, but he remained behind.

Maybe I *hoped* for him to give me chase. It would have meant he cared for me. Did I want that? I didn't know what I wanted beyond saving my people from slaughter.

I continued onward, only using the sounds ahead as a guide. The fighting couldn't be too far off. I didn't have weapons on me, nor any armor. This was something far out of my element, but it was also a tack I believed my father would have taken.

"Find the local unit commander. Have him call off the automaton units," Ivan said as I left.

At least he'd done something, even if he wasn't chasing after me. I kept my pace. Slowing down might cause Ivan to think seizing me would be an option. I would fight tooth and nail if he tried it.

My path took me off the road and into the forest. Thick trees made it difficult to see. Darkness covered the forest floor from their shadows. I'd only been in Loveridge briefly before when the world was new to me, and the rapid changes in scenery overstimulated me. I hardly remembered the area, except thinking that the long planks of the airship were a wall around the town. I hadn't been able to see much or get my bearings. Nor would I have much time to this time around.

All I could do was to keep moving forward. My plans would work out. They had to. I had my von Monocle luck... or was it giant's blood luck? I had so much to think about with Ivan's revelations of my genealogy. Who was I? My father would know. He remembered my mother better than anyone. I wished I could ask him if Ivan were telling the truth.

Roots and rocks protruded with each step on the forest floor, making it difficult to keep balance. I wasn't dressed for a jaunt into the wilderness and found myself stumbling several times along the walk toward the sounds of the fighting. I also had to travel farther than I'd originally thought—the sounds carried deep into the forest.

I started to doubt myself. Maybe it would have been better to wait until daylight. What if the Rislandians shot on sight? I wouldn't blame them for being jumpy. I became lost in thought, shoulders tensing though I continued to push myself forward.

My toe caught in a tree root.

I stumbled forward, pedaling my feet try to regain my balance. My hand scraped against the trunk of a tree, but I couldn't stop my forward momentum.

I slammed into something hard. It hit right at my cheekbone, pain flaring in my face. I tried to wrap my arms around whatever I'd run into, bracing myself. It lurched backward but settled, smacking into me again on the way back toward me. Metal hitting my chest. It knocked the wind out of me, causing me to gasp for air.

When my eyes adjusted, I could see the shining metal of the flat automaton face.

Unable to help myself, I screamed.

It was irrational. The thing was just a hunk of metal standing there, and from the looks of it, Ivan had deactivated the machine. It wasn't moving at all.

To compound my problems, a bullet whizzed into the automaton's face, ricocheting off of it. Metal on metal caused sparking. I dropped to the ground.

More bullets whizzed toward me. After several shots hit the metal above me, the automaton fell backward, crashing to the ground. Fortunately, I was on the other side of it.

"Stop firing!" I shouted.

"Who's there?" came a man's voice from the forest.

"It's Zaira von Monocle," I said.

"A woman?" Another voice asked. Footsteps came forward, crackling with the leaves and small sticks on the ground. I hoped they weren't jumpy.

One man came up to me, grabbing by the arm. He helped me to my feet.

"Baron?" The voice asked. Even in the darkness, I could make out his features. The silhouette had a muscular upper body and a finely chiseled face.

"Sergeant Wright?" I asked. Unable to help myself, I hugged him.

"Oof," he said, patting me on the back with his free hand, keeping his rifle off to the side in the other. "What, by Malaky, are you doing out here?"

I pulled back and looked up at the man who had led my airship commandos for the last year. Two other Rislandian soldiers came forward to flank him, rifles in their hands. "I came to stop the Wyranth from killing any more Rislandians," I said.

Wright put his hand up with a closed fist. "It's all right. She's with us. Let's get you back to camp."

I followed him and the other soldiers. During the walk, no more soldiers fired bullets. Had I successfully stopped the battle? Only time would tell.

CHAPTER 19

AT THE CAMP, First Sergeant Wright gave me a blanket to cover my shoulders and a warm cup of tea. He said it wasn't the best, but the boiled water was the cleanest to drink while on the lines. The warmth of the fire made me happy. I enjoyed the comradery of sitting on the logs with the other Rislandian soldiers.

Despite my relative contentment, the soldiers around me looked drained, with far too many frowns amongst. Their morale had dropped to new lows, even compared to what I'd seen in the worst of the fighting. They'd lost their will to fight.

I did my best to lighten their moods by introducing myself, thanking them for their service. I'd had some practice at morale building in recent months, while I had been trapped dirtside.

A group of soldiers stayed near me, and we exchanged stories. Most of them wanted to know how my life had been. They'd heard I was traded to the Wyranth in exchange for help with the airship. Their unit had a plan to bust through the lines to rescue me.

I laughed. "I don't need rescuing. It was my own decision."

"Why?" One of the men asked.

I looked him in the eye.

"Sometimes, a person has to make sacrifices for the greater good. My going to the Wyranth Empire will allow Rislandia's airship to fly again. That's an advantage I can't let go to waste," I said.

"Hear hear," a man said, holding a canteen which he drank from. Even from where I sat, the pungent smell of his drink wafted over to me. The man smiled. "I don't know if you remember me. Corporal Tyson. I helped you and your father secure a bomb from Rislandia City's industrial district."

I returned the smile. "I remember you. Thank you very much for your assistance."

Tyson nodded. "I like what you're sayin' about sacrifice. Lot of us here have sacrificed a lot, and it's nice to hear the nobles have the same sentiment, even in these times."

The others muttered agreements around me.

I'd gotten good at saying the right thing in front of the men, making sure they kept their morale up. It's not that I was trying to manipulate them, but if I could help them feel better about their fight, it would go a long way.

"Not sure it'll do a lick of good against these machine men, though," Tyson said.

I frowned. "That'll be the second part of what I'm doing. I'll have the ear of the Iron Emperor. I made them stop firing tonight."

Tyson glanced behind him, toward the infantry line. He listened intently. "You're right. There's no more fighting. Huh."

"He going to give our lands back?" Sergeant Wright asked.

"I'm working on it," I said, taking another sip of tea. "This ceasefire is the first of it. I'm hoping I can get him to pull back his people from Loveridge."

"What if he doesn't listen to you?" Tyson asked.

I shrugged. "All I can do is try."

"S'pose you're right," Tyson said.

Silence lingered, the fire flickering in front of us. Despite the blanket and my warm tea, I shivered from a cold welling inside of me. Part of me wished I'd find Ethan here and be able to run into his arms. But he had his mission. His talent wouldn't be wasted by the knights in an infantry skirmish at the line.

Was I getting into a glum mood because of the others around me? I tried to lift their spirits, but their overall sentiment couldn't help but bring my energy down. I hadn't thought through all entailed by running across the line. What was I to do now? Go back to Ivan?

My goal had been to stop the fighting. I'd done that, but how long would it last? And what about other battle locations down the line? We needed something more, a nationwide truce. Ivan would have to give up more than he was willing to bargain to make it happen, though. I wasn't sure if he'd be reasonable about it.

At least I'd gotten to know him a little better. The key to him was to push him in the direction he was excited. He had an intense focus when he wanted something, and he would ignore anything other than that. If I could keep his attention on these crystals... perhaps I could coax him on an expedition somewhere, putting a pause to hostilities here.

It was as good an idea as any. I finished the rest of my tea. The soldiers looked tired, ready to go to sleep. I felt the same. "I have a plan, but I'm going to need some time to work it out." I glanced to Sergeant Wright. "Do you think you can help?"

Sergeant Wright nodded. "Of course. Anything for you, Baronette."

I enjoyed hearing the nickname. "Baronette" used to bother me, as it wasn't my technical title, but the troops meant it as a term of endearment. I missed my old crew so much.

"Okay. First, don't do anything to break the ceasefire here. I'm going to do all I can to get Ivan to pull those automatons back, and then hopefully retreat from Loveridge," I said.

Tyson chuckled. "If that's all it took, we shoulda sent you over the border earlier."

The uncomfortable silence came back. Most of the soldiers weren't sure if I'd find it funny. I'm sure with the alcohol he'd consumed, he didn't mean to imply I was worth more as a prisoner than here, but it's the way it came out.

For the sake of the troops, I decided to roll with it. "Maybe so," I said, trying to sound in good spirits. "But I'll need a messenger to go to Rislandia City as well. We'll have to take back a message to King Malaky that we are going to push for peace. We'll have to make some compromises, but it'll be better than prolonged battles."

"I'm afraid we can't do that," Sergeant Wright said.

Was he defying me? Did compromise cause the problems? Had Rislandia soldiers become so bloodthirsty they wouldn't lay down arms against the Wyranth? I understood it was hard. I wanted vengeance for all I'd lost, but I also saw the destructive path our nation would spiral into if we continued a war, especially against Ivan's new automatons. The death toll would be tremendous. "Why not?" My words came out meeker then I would have liked.

"Then you don't know." Wright's eyes darkened, becoming deadly serious.

"No." I was so confused. All the soldiers looked at me like I was crazy.

Wright reached over and took my hand. It was in a friendly way, not trying to make some move on me. He squeezed my hand, almost like a brother or father would have done. "King Malaky's dead."

CHAPTER 20

I FORGOT HOW to breathe.

As embarrassing as it is to admit, I grew dizzy and fainted.

Minutes later, the soldiers roused me with smelling salts, Corporal Tyson patting lightly on my face. "Baronette?" He asked, taking to the name.

"I'm awake," I said, voice cracking. Weakness consumed my body from lack of sleep, and I had the worst dryness in my throat.

King Malaky had died. It was so unreal, even though he'd looked so frail before.

I thought back, recalling my last encounters with him. I wished I'd hugged him or told him how much he meant to me. But I'd been so singularly focused on this mission. I couldn't do anything else. At least he had wanted me to pursue marrying Ivan in order to retrieve the airship plans, but still...

"I need some time to think," I said. "Can we sleep before we make any decisions? Do you have an extra bed roll?" The last thing I wanted to do was to go back to Ivan. I wanted to be alone. To cry over the king.

So many thoughts spun through my head. Ivan would come up with some scheme because of this, no doubt. Rislandia would be in turmoil. Or would it? Princess Reina would take over for her father, but could she handle the responsibilities of being Queen?

She had to be too young for the position, too green. I didn't have faith in her like I had in King Malaky. But was it because I didn't like her? As much as she'd always been kind to me, we didn't have the best relationship. It was awkward. Her and James had become very close. It hadn't been long ago when everyone presumed I would be the one to marry him. I didn't begrudge her the relationship... at least I didn't *think* I did. Maybe it wasn't so simple.

I shook my head. These thoughts weren't helping anything. If I had some personal problem with her, it wouldn't affect her abilities to lead. Besides, she had the best advisors in the world in my father, Talyen, and Mr. du Gearsmith. It would be fine.

But the King's death would still be a powerful symbol in this war.

It meant I had to redouble my effort to bring an end to hostilities between us and the Wyranth. If we didn't, Ivan would take even greater advantage than his acquisition of the automatons.

Despite my desire to run away, I had to return to Ivan as quickly as possible. I couldn't hide this from him. Being forthright would build trust and help me toward my goals—keeping Rislandia safe.

The next morning, the sun trickled over the horizon, glittering across my eyes to wake me. I readied myself and let the Rislandian soldiers know where I had to go and made my way back across the line. The automatons lined the forest, the same places they were the prior evening when Ivan shut them down. Dead, standing in the forest in the daylight—a creepy sight. I wondered how much these machines had the ability to think or feel, if they did at all. Ivan didn't let me in on the secrets of how they worked.

It took me an hour's walk to make it back to Loveridge. Wyranth soldiers spotted me, and ushered me to the inn where Ivan had made a makeshift residence.

Loveridge had more activity during the day, with men working carts and moving through the streets. I didn't see many women or children, but then, if I didn't have to be out and about with an automaton army looming, I wouldn't be, either.

Inside, I found Ivan seated on a couch within the main common area. Several Wyranth soldiers buzzed about him. He read reports from them, focused. He took several moments before looking up at me. "Ah, Zaira. You returned quickly. I see you were successful in getting the Rislandians to ceasefire." He wrinkled his forehead. "Is there something wrong? You look like you've seen a ghost."

"Yes, there is," I said, helping myself to a seat across from him. "There's a lot to discuss, but the most important thing is I'm going to have to go back to Rislandia City, at least for a little while."

"Giving up on your airship?" Ivan asked.

I shook my head. "No, I'll return. It's just..." I let out a deep breath. Should I really be the one to break the news? In some ways, I doubted it, but I needed Ivan to trust me if I were going to influence him in earnest. "King Malaky is dead."

For the first time, Ivan looked truly surprised. "Pardon?"

"You heard me," I said. I wanted to burst into tears, but I couldn't. I had to keep myself together.

"That is a shocking development." Ivan paused, frowning. "I'm going to have to reevaluate recent tactics."

"You still need to deescalate the war," I said. "Enough people have died."

"Of course. I keep my word. Perhaps the incoming queen will be more amicable to letting the Wyranth have some of the tillable area north of the Border River and we can end this conflict."

Why did he make me want to hit him so much? King Malaky was dead and he worried about the farmland he seized? Every time I thought he was close to human, Ivan showed he had no soul, no concern for anything outside his wild schemes. It was maddening.

"I suppose I'll have to let you return to Rislandia City. It will delay the wedding plans, but we have plenty of time. Would you do something for me first?"

"What?" I asked, crossing my arms over my chest.

Ivan reached into his pocket and produced a small object. It looked like a rock, jagged, with several dents in it. He held it open in his palm. "If you recall, this was the crystal I had powering the machine. The ancient stories, however, didn't require a machine to operate it. I am hoping you'll try an experiment. Join hands with me, and see if we can activate the earth crystal with our wills."

That was what he wanted of me? If that's all it took for me to return to my people, to see how they were doing, to grieve with them, I would gladly do it. I stepped forward.

He patted the couch beside him.

I sat. "Okay. So what do we do?"

"Take my hand, over the crystal."

I did so. The jagged surface of the rock pressed against my palm, though it didn't cut me. Ivan entwined his fingers with mine in a surprising move. My first instinct was to recoil, but I stopped myself from pulling back. His hand was cool, and he stared at me with his intense blue eyes.

"Now what?" I asked.

"Try to connect with the crystal."

"How?"

"Focus. Breathe. Think of the crystal. See if you can feel it. I've spent months doing just this. I can sense a resonance from it, almost like a vibration." He closed his eyes and breathed in through his nose.

I tried to follow his lead, breathing slowly like him. My mind whirled, though. I couldn't stop to focus on the crystal. All I could think of was King Malaky, my father, the others back home. They must be devastated. I should have been there with them.

I tried harder to think about the crystal in our hands. I felt it. It stayed cool, despite the warmth of our skin. How could I connect with it? It didn't vibrate at all, despite what Ivan told me.

We must have looked ridiculous, sitting there hand in hand, in the middle of an inn in the middle of a war zone, our eyes closed. Still, nothing happened. If there was a way to connect with these substances to make use of them, I didn't have the capability. My eyes fluttered open.

Ivan's eyes stayed closed a moment longer, and then he opened them. He straightened his fingers and pulled his hand back, glancing down at the crystal. "I'm not sure what else we're supposed to do."

"Something else to research for when I get back," I said.

Ivan nodded, eyes peering at me curiously. "You've been rather accepting of every circumstance I've thrown in front of you."

"What else can I do?" I asked, shrugging.

"Merely an observation. I half expected more fight from you."

"I've grown up a lot since we met last."

Those blue eyes seemed to soften. "That you have." He inclined his head. "Go do what you have to do and return to me quickly."

I stood, not sure what else we should do. Were we supposed to shake hands? Hug? None of it felt right, though I stood in front of him an awkward silence. "You should pull your troops from Loveridge. Show sincerity in ending this war."

"I'll consider it," he said.

Now it was my turn to be surprised. I expected more fight from him. Were these crystals truly worth this much to him? I didn't understand. But then, I didn't need to. I had to do my duty. "Thank you," I said, turning for the exit.

CHAPTER 21

THE NEXT DAY, I'd made it into Rislandia City with a Wyranth driver. Ivan had let me take a horseless carriage for the journey, generous as ever. I would be returning to the Wyranth capital in four days' time, enough for me to attend a funeral procession for King Malaky and to grieve with my friends.

Instead of bringing me comfort, the Rislandian flags flying at half-mast over the walls of the city only brought me a sense of loss. The towers stood, our loyal city guards keeping watch. The city had lost its luster as of late, with our population down since the invasion.

Black cloths lined the tops of the city walls, which continued into the city streets inside. Shops all had black hanging, all signaling their mourning of the passing king. It made the city feel oppressive, glum. My mood hadn't been the best. I was stuck—with Ivan, with my life, more isolated than ever, and nothing went my way. I hadn't even rightly been able to celebrate any of my major victories because even greater losses kept accompanying them.

Would I ever be able to find happiness again?

I silently chastised myself for having such a petty concern in the midst of the death of our king, but it still loomed in my mind. Why not? When was the last time I cared for myself?

I sighed as our horseless carriage carried us through the streets and toward the palace. City guards lined the streets, holding candles in vigil for King Malaky.

He had been the kindest king I ever could have imagined. This wasn't fair. We fought so hard, and we'd lost our true champion.

Several people waited outside the palace to greet me, including Talyen, baby Lilly in her arms, and Marina. Ivan must have announced when I'd be returning. I gave them hugs, but none of us spoke while we walked. What could we possibly say?

We ended up in the war room inside the palace, where my father sat at his desk, with several other military officers gathered around. A large model map of Rislandia rested on a table near to him. Everyone kept working hard, yet silence hung in the room. Someone had to break the tension.

"Hi," I said.

My father looked up. He had bags under his eyes. Judging from the redness of them, he'd obviously been crying, though he wouldn't admit it if I asked. His hair ruffled in different directions and curled behind his ears. Stubble peppered his face, with more grey and white than I remembered. "Zaira," he said, standing.

I shuffled behind his desk and gave him a big hug, clinging to him like I had when I was a little girl. I'd lost him then. I knew what it was like to lose someone and have it impact my life.

King Malaky had been more to my father than just the king, he'd been my father's best friend. The two of them grew up together, spent time together in leisure as well as for work. Both of them had lost their wives to the terrible disease that passed through the kingdom so many years ago. I couldn't imagine how he felt.

He hugged me tightly. I rested my head against his chest.

My father's familiar musky scent washed over me, comforting me. It reminded me of being much younger, when he would return from his airship adventures and bring me presents. He would always have something for me, and I got to guess what it was and where it came from. This time, his presence was enough of a gift for me.

Eventually, he pulled back and returned to his seat. "As much as it would be nice to spend time together, we should discuss what you learned while you were in the Wyranth Empire. I expect they'll be redoubling their efforts to disrupt our kingdom with the passing of King Malaky," he said.

I told him everything I saw, including Ivan's strange fixation on the crystals. My father watched intently as I recounted the story, though I could tell he lacked focus. He appeared even more downtrodden than when I'd rescued him from a Wyranth prison.

"Crystals," my father shook his head.

"You don't believe it?" I asked.

"Oh, I've seen enough in this world that I'll believe anything, especially after you witnessed the power of them firsthand. We'll have to get our intelligence agents working on finding one of these crystals so we can get Harkerpal and the others testing it. Maybe we can find a way to get you out of there..."

I bit my lip. "I think I can do better inside the Wyranth Empire. Ivan stopped his attack on our men at Loveridge because I told him to. And he said he'd consider pulling back the troops entirely."

"You can't seriously trust that man." The features on my father's face tightened.

"He's not dishonest."

My father just stared at me.

"When has he lied?"

"How about when he sent you on a mission to another continent in the name of our own security, leaving our kingdom without an airship to defend it?" My father's tone held venom.

"He told me it hadn't been his intention."

"More lies!"

I frowned. It wouldn't matter. Nothing I could say would get through to him. His hatred of Ivan kept him from being rational about the man. Not that I liked Ivan very much. I just... respected him some, and understood him a lot better than I had before. In a lot of ways, he was doing what he thought was best for his people, like we were trying to do for ours. His means were aggressive and hurt ours, however. My father could never comprehend it, but I understood the good I could do. It was more important than anything I could do in Rislandia.

"You don't have to trust him, but trust me," I said.

My father's lips tightened but then he leaned back in his chair. "I'm sorry I snapped at you. I hate that man. He's responsible for the death of my best friend, not to mention so many others."

"I know," I said.

He sighed. "I don't want to lose you to him too."

"You won't. I promise. I'm going to do everything I can for Rislandia. That's the whole point. He's tactical. If I can get him to see that there's more advantages to being our friend than our enemy..."

"It's wishful thinking."

"Isn't that what people told you when you first started adventuring?"

My father laughed. "You're stubborn."

"Apple doesn't fall far from the tree." I shrugged. "Everyone always tells me how much I'm like you. Except Ivan."

"Yes, interesting about your mother. I knew her small kingdom had a prestigious lineage, but I had no idea the extent. I'll have to see if some of the royal historians can look into these claims. Giant's blood. It's all so fantastical, though given my experience in the world, I have to believe it's true," he said, before glancing toward the table map of Rislandia. "I need to come up with a plan to handle these automatons. It's a shame this resistance presents itself now of all times. We don't have the resources to do much to help them."

"I figured as much," I said.

He nodded. "You always had a good head on your shoulders. It doesn't mean we can't give them some encouragement all the same. I think it would be a bad idea to have you contact them from inside the Wyranth capital, however. If the Iron Emperor believes you're subverting him, it would mean your head. No matter how enamored with you he is, or whatever his pet project, he's still a tyrant."

Having spent time with him, I may have been biased, but I didn't think he was quite as bad as my father made him out to be. I still wanted him to change more, though, and I would make it happen. "You should take a few days off to rest. I don't think Ivan will be making any advances in the meantime. He wants me to come back."

My father winced. "I wish you wouldn't call him by his name."

"Why?"

"It humanizes him."

"He's a person."

Another impasse. Another awkward silence. My father shook his head. "But you're right. Enough talk for now. There's so much going on I can barely handle it all. We should enjoy each other's company..."

The unsaid words *while there's still time* lingered in the air. "Yes. Let's."

"I wish I was in better spirits, Zaira."

"You will be. You've every right to grieve. I feel it too," I said.

My father stood and circled the table again. He embraced me and kissed me on the top of my head. "I love you so much, and I'm proud of you. You know that?"

The words made my whole body tingle. I understood, but tears filled my eyes all the same. "I do. I love you too."

We stood there holding each other for a long time. No one else in the room stared or bothered, but my father pulled back, inhaling a deep breath. "Let's get you something to eat. You've got to be famished."

My stomach rumbled. I hadn't thought of it since I'd been there. I'd been too focused on King Malaky and my father to even think about food, but it sounded good. "Okay."

We left the war room and made our way into a residential wing of the palace where my father stayed, along with Talyen and baby Lilly. A servant opened the double doors to his quarters, which were comprised of a large open room with lavish dark wooden furniture, gold ornamentation, and a beautiful crimson rug. It was a sitting room enough for a king, but then, it was in the royal palace. "The perks of being the chief military strategist," my father had told me when he first moved in.

I still preferred the cramped quarters of the airship.

Dinner looked amazing. The palace chefs provided food on par with what I'd been served at the Wyranth capital, but at the same time, I couldn't bring myself to eat much. Despite being happy to see everyone again, I found it difficult to keep in a good mood. I wanted to make these moments count, in case these were the last I spent with my friends and family, but I couldn't find a way to lift my spirits. From the tired looks in the eyes of the others, except for baby Lilly who had no idea what was going on, they all felt the same.

Could we ever bring ourselves back to a state of normalcy? All I wanted was for people to stop dying, and for this war to go away.

CHAPTER 22

THREE MORE DAYS passed while I waited for the procession and funeral for King Malaky. I was back to my place before, where I had little to do to be useful to my colleagues or country. At least I got to see Toby again. While staying in the palace, I got to see him quite a bit. The servants didn't to like the little, furry tyrant, but Lilly sure did, and even Talyen grew a fondness for his scampering about.

In some ways, I longed to be back in Ivan's palace. At least he showed me interesting things. I could be working with the crystals, trying to figure out if there were some innate ability in me to use them, but instead I was stuck.

I grew restless in addition to my sorrow. All I wanted was to move on, to do something productive or helpful, to find some sort of purpose. It made the days drag on so long.

The palace servants rushed around in disarray the whole time. They had to organize a procession throughout the city which was to end in the open courtyard at the front of the king's main chamber—or the Queen's main chamber now. The servants buzzed around, less attentive than usual as they engaged in their work.

They kept Princess Reina in seclusion. I had no idea what was going on in her head. It had to have been hard. I remembered thinking my father was dead. It may have been a bit tougher on me without the vast support network of the royal palace around me, to be honest, but I still sympathized.

Despite my prior rivalries with her, I went to find her in the palace. A stack of paperwork towered over her in a small chamber on the east wing of the palace. She curled over a table with Mr. du Gearsmith and a couple of other advisors I didn't recognize.

"You have to sign off on the taxation forms," Mr. du Gearsmith said.

"But I don't know what it means."

"There will be time for that later."

"I can't just sign things without understanding them."

Mr. du Gearsmith sighed, but his face was one of understanding and patience. "In ordinary times, you would be correct. For now, we need to keep this kingdom running through the transition while you get acclimated. There won't be time for going over these smaller items in detail enough for you to comprehend. Understanding will come later, through repetition."

Princess Reina threw her head back. "I need a break."

Mr. du Gearsmith caught my eye, and then frowned. "Perhaps that's for the best. You have company. Let us resume in, say, half an hour?"

Reina looked up. "Oh, Zaira. I didn't see you there." She cocked her head. "Wait. You're here?"

I bowed my head before her. "I wanted to come and offer my condolences, uh... your Majesty." It was odd saying that to her, but it was also the right thing to say.

The advisors cleared out of the room to give us space.

"I suppose I'll have to get used to being called that. You can look at me, it's fine." She ran a finger through her golden locks. "This has been the worst few days of my life."

"I understand," I said.

Reina frowned. "You do, don't you?" She let out a deep breath. "It's even harder with the responsibilities of a kingdom. I had no idea how many facets there were to running a government, and then there's all of the requests from the peasantry... is it even appropriate to call them that anymore? I know the term upsets a few people."

I shrugged.

"Those are the kinds of things I need to be aware of. If I misspeak it could destroy morale, or cause a revolt, or who knows. My father always tried to tell me to watch and learn, but it's not the same when you're looking over the shoulder of someone making all of the decisions." She slapped her hand down on the desk, causing papers to fly from the force of it. "Ugh!"

"You'll get the hang of it. People love you," I said. At least James loved her. He was strong and decisive. As soon as he returned from this mission, I was sure it would go better for her.

"Thank you, Zaira," Reina said. "I'm sorry to lay all that on you. You've always been such a good friend to me."

I had? I blinked. "It's nothing."

"It's everything. I shouldn't let you return to that awful empire, but I understand why my father made the decision to let you go. We need this war to stop now more than ever."

"I know. I'll do everything I can."

Reina slipped her lithe frame around the desk. She ventured over and gave me a soft hug. "Thank you for everything you do. You're an inspiration. I shouldn't worry about all this paperwork when you're sacrificing your whole life for me."

I wanted to argue that it wasn't for her, but I figured it wouldn't be a good time. "It's too bad you couldn't have a few days."

"I know. But it's as Mr. du Gearsmith said, 'the kingdom won't stop.' Here, let me get you some tea and you can tell me what's going on with you."

She called in a servant, who then returned with tea and biscuits a few minutes later. We chatted pleasantries, and Reina's spirits lightened over the conversation. At least I could help her in a small way. I sipped my tea. "How do you sign papers anyway?" I asked. "Queen Malaky?"

Reina shook her head. "They wanted me to, but I'm going by Queen Reina the First. Mr. du Gearsmith about had a heart attack when I told him. He went pale and started rambling at me about traditions."

"What did you say?"

"I said things change and he'd better get used to it. He didn't fight after that. It's kind of nice having ultimate authority."

I remembered when Mr. du Gearsmith first brought me to the palace and lectured me about traditions maintained here. He made me wear that strange poofy attire while keeping my eyes cast low, not talking until I was spoken to. He definitely had the feeling of the old guard. It would do good to have Reina loosen him up some. "I like it. Reina the First... Reina the Great?" I smiled at her.

"Let's not get ahead of ourselves." She chuckled.

We had a few more minutes to ourselves before the advisors came back in. They hurried me out of the room so Reina could get back to work. I told her I'd see her at the procession the next day, but she had returned her focus to her papers by the time I did.

The rest of the day went slowly. I walked about the palace grounds, surveying the training knights, remembering when it was James out there learning how to use a sword for the first time. How the world spun so quickly... and how we all changed in the blink of an eye. The thought depressed me. I had to pull myself out of this funk.

I wasn't able to pull from my funk for the rest of the day. Finally, feeling down and tired, I retired early, without dinner.

The next morning, I woke up to trumpets blaring in a rhythmic military manner. Talyen poked her head in my room. "Hurry up, Zaira. You overslept. The procession is beginning soon."

I hurried to slip a formal gown over my head and rushed out the door with Talyen.

Visitors filled the palace. Navigating the corridors proved difficult, but Talyen grabbed my hand. She moved with a purpose, and the people naturally parted for her. I envied her confidence and vowed to remember how she made people do what she wanted by acting in charge. It didn't hurt that she held one of the highest ranks in the kingdom.

We eventually made it to some side doors which led into the main courtyard. We exited the steps onto the raised platform before the archway that led into the palace. As in the corridors, people swarmed. I'd never seen more gathered masses of people in my life. They stretched down the road as far as I could see.

With us on the platform stood several dignitaries in formal attire—dresses and suits. Some I recognized as various nobility from around Rislandia, along with ambassadors from Atrebla and Nyanzi who had permanent stations within the kingdom.

An honor guard of the Grand Rislandian Army stood in their dress uniforms, brass buttons down the right sides of their dark crimson tunics, with their base-gray pants. They wore flat, fuzzed black hats with a golden pin of the Crest of Malaky in the center. Each of them held rifles, pointed toward the air.

A band comprised of military members played behind them. The musicians played several brass instruments, trumpets and others I didn't recognize. I hadn't been trained in music. I liked listening to it when I could, but my upbringing didn't allow me much time other than hearing my mother sing to me or listening to an occasional fiddler at a harvest festival. Once I'd moved to Rislandia, I had even less time to enjoy the arts. It made me think about Ivan's pride in how the Wyranth prioritized culture. Perhaps I should add a little more of it to my life.

The band played a complex and sobering tune, with rough staccato notes. It fit the mood perfectly as the crowd quieted to listen. It allowed us all to reflect on King Malaky and mourn.

Several women cried. I did my best to hold it in. Talyen kept her lips tight, looking stoic. How did she maintain such composure all the time?

Princess Reina seated herself, beside several members of the nobility who surrounded her. She wore a black dress with a small veil over her face, concealing most of her expression, except for her frowning lips, bright red with lipstick.

My father stood in front of a podium. A large device stood in front of him, amplifying his words in a tube so people could hear from a distance. It made his voice sound strange, almost higher than usual. He wore a military dress uniform as well, which looked good on him.

The music stopped. "Good day, Rislandia City," my father said. He cleared his throat, struggling with words, but he held himself mostly together. "King Malaky was the best of us. He meant more than just a symbol to Rislandia as king. He was our heart, our soul. Like many who are here with me, he was more than a king to me, he was a friend. We come to do honor to him today, and to remember what we fight for as Rislandians. King Malaky stood for truth, for courage, and for self-determination. He gave us more than any monarch in the history of this world, and it was more than an honor to serve for him."

My father paused, either to catch his breath or to compose himself, I wasn't sure. "But we have to remember that there is still a lot to do for this kingdom. He may no longer be here with us in physical form, but his spirit lives on within all of us. It's our duty to see through the initiatives that he started, and to restore Rislandia to its full glory. I call on you to stand tall with me and to be proud Rislandians for King Malaky. He wanted nothing more than for all of you to be the best versions of yourselves you could be."

He paused again and dabbed at his eyes with his handkerchief. "On the airship, we had a saying, 'for steam and country', which we said to remind ourselves of all of the rapid developments we'd seen in Rislandia these last years, and that we were privileged to be able to defend them. I urge you to keep strong, maintain your heart, and fight your hardest—whether it be tilling in the fields, reconstructing our buildings, doing battle proper, or even in raising your children—do it for *king* and country. Do it for the memory of King Malaky, may he ever be in our hearts."

A rousing cheer came from the crowd. It continued on into the city. The sound of so many people in agreement, unanimous in one cause brought a warmth to my heart. This kingdom was worth fighting for, and so was everyone in it. My father's words rang true, and I would do my best in my duty, as well. I wouldn't lose hope.

It was exactly what I needed to hear, and perhaps what everyone else here needed, too. My father told stories of King Malaky and himself as boys and then stepped from the podium and the amplifying device. Princess Reina stood and gave him a hug, and the band started to play again.

A procession slowly pushed down the busy street, with an elegant wooden coffin carried by military personnel. The crowd parted as the men marched to the rhythm of the song playing, a somber tune with a pretty melody. The coffin holders came to the podium and stopped. The military men on the platform stepped forward in unison, and each fired three shots into the air in honor of King Malaky. A long moment of silence fell over the crowd as we all made peace with our fallen king.

A woman in a long, crimson gown stepped forward and lit a big candle in front of the coffin, and then Princess Reina laid a wreath atop it. Music began again, a softer tune as it signified the end of the procession. The crowd slowly began to disburse.

Princess Reina bawled, collapsing in front of the coffin containing her fallen father. Others moved to console her. All I could do was watch.

It was the end of an era in Rislandia. I could only hope the next one would be as bright.

CHAPTER 23

THE FINAL DAY of my trip passed as we mourned over the loss of our king. Princess—no, *Queen* Reina seemed to acclimate to her roles of handling disputes and paperwork, as well as learning to be more tactful. "I've decided to start calling peasants *workers*—they seem to like it better. I just have to train my mind for it," she told me while passing in the corridors of the palace one day.

I'd hoped Ethan and James would return before I had to depart again, but they were still off on their mission halfway around the world. It was probably for the better, because Ethan would try to convince me not to go back to the Wyranth Empire, something I had to do.

After the procession, I found myself in better spirits. Most of the palace also seemed less glum. Life had to go on. We all had to pick ourselves up and put one foot in front of the other.

The goodbyes came a little easier this time. I visited everyone I knew in Rislandia City, and then met with Queen Reina and my father over strategic matters. They wanted to know where the automatons were being built, and impressed upon me a map of the Wyranth capital. I didn't know where it was based on my last experience, but I would remember the next time I saw it and bring information back to them.

They formulated plans for having the knights infiltrate and destroy the Wyranth factories. Something I hoped wouldn't be necessary—there would be so much loss of life involved.

Finally, I had to depart, and so I said goodbyes again, giving hugs and kisses to my family. Queen Reina walked me to the horseless carriage, where a Wyranth driver sat in the front seat ready to take me south. He had been put up on the ambassadorial wing while waiting for me.

We travelled, this time much less eventfully, as I'd been told the Grand Rislandian Army did a sweep for looters and robbers along the road after my last incident. We passed the demarcation zone without incident as well.

When we passed Loveridge, several of Ivan's automatons still stood out in the fields, motionless, dead. The ceasefire had held through the funeral, and hopefully with my influence, it would continue and Rislandians would be allowed to regain their land again. The driver sped down the road, though it still took most of the day to get down into Wyranth territory. I didn't mind. I found myself coming to enjoy watching the scenery go by at a much slower pace than the airship allowed. With the wind blowing through my hair, I could almost imagine I was aboard the *Liliana*, giving orders, getting ready for some adventure. Would I be able to fly again?

It was a big question, and it hung on my heart even heavier than the prospect of marrying Ivan. I wanted to take to the skies more than anything, and do so with my crew. I sighed as the horizon turned to a pink and orange color in the early evening.

We entered the city with little fanfare. Automatons guarded the city, more of them than before, as they'd been multiplying. Human guards let down the gates to allow us entry. We passed through the streets and up to Ivan's palace.

The sight of it brought me a great surprise.

At the palace stood an honor guard of Wyranth soldiers, standing at attention in their dark uniforms with their pointed, metal helmets. Five lined each side of the entryway to the palace, which had a crimson carpet rolled in front, covered in red rose petals.

To the right stood a quartet of musicians with stringed instruments. They played a lively, happy tune.

My driver stopped the horseless carriage, turning off the motor, which allowed me to hear the musicians much better, and also removed the aether fuel exhaust from the air, allowing me to smell the freshness of the roses.

I could get used to being greeted this way. It was flattering, a much better reception than the last time I'd been here. What was Ivan's game?

The driver opened my car door, escorting me out of it and onto the red carpet.

The doors to the palace flew open, held by dual servants inside. Ivan stepped forward, wearing an elegant dark suit which accented his tall, lithe figure. His eyes met mine immediately, and he smiled.

Then, he strode forward and dropped to one knee in front of me.

Startled, I stopped in the path. I couldn't imagine Ivan bowing for anyone, let alone me. In fact, I was surprised that there wasn't a protocol in place to force me to show my deference to him.

"Zaira, welcome back," Ivan said, inclining his head toward me once again.

"What's this about?" I asked softly, the music crescendoing behind me.

"It came to my attention that you didn't receive the proper greeting for an empress when we last met. I want to assure you that the Wyranth do not take these measures lightly, nor are we unappreciative of the bride of our people." He held up one of his hands, closed in a fist, and then turned it so his palm faced upward. His fingers straightened, revealing a finely engraved white-gold band with a large diamond set within it. "Please accept this gift to commence our formal engagement."

The ring was so beautiful I forgot to breathe. I couldn't believe he'd done this for me. Where was the cold and calculating emperor I'd interacted with so many times before? He'd always told me culture was important to him, so I supposed this scene was an element of demonstrating it.

What else could I do but to accept? So many eyes rested on me, I didn't dare react poorly, not to mention the whole gesture was... sweet. I couldn't believe any of my senses. I'd worried that I'd be treated as a prisoner when with the Wyranth, but it seemed those fears were unwarranted.

Could it be I wouldn't hate being married to Ivan?

He raised his hand forward to remind me he still held the ring, palm outstretched toward me.

In my shock I'd forgotten to react. I carefully took the ring between my fingers, then slipped it onto the fourth finger of my left hand.

It fit perfectly, not too tight, nor was it at risk of falling off. How had he obtained my measurements? It reminded me that there was always more to Ivan than met the eye. He paid attention to detail, had a craftiness about him.

Once the ring was on my finger, he stood and took my hand, surveying it. "The empress's jewel looks beautiful on you."

My face turned hot. Malaky help me, I liked being treated like royalty. But I had to keep my dignity about me. I was here for a purpose, to ensure Rislandia's safety. Even still, this wasn't a bad means by which to do it at all.

"I have dinner prepared for you, if you're willing to join me?" Ivan asked.

I nodded.

He kept ahold of my hand, turning and leading me into the palace.

I'd been craving a crazy adventure, and this certainly fit the bill, just not the way I'd anticipated.

CHAPTER 24

IVAN CALLED ME into his sitting room. He spoke with another Wyranth as I entered, and dismissed the other man when I arrived.

"Ah, Zaira. Thank you for joining me," he said, standing. His eyes flickered toward my hand, plainly curious if I still wore the ring he'd bestowed on me the prior day.

I did. The band added a strange weight to my hand, and it itched because my skin wasn't used to having something pressing against it.

I kept it on regardless of the irritation. It was pretty, and moreover, gave me an air of authority around the palace. The servants became a little more deferential toward me than before, something in the way they paused to bow their heads in respect when I passed, or asked me if there were something they could be doing for me.

It was one of the ways I would gain influence here and make a change.

Ivan grinned at me. "One of the things I like about you is your ability to understand the tactical situations and adapt. It's truly remarkable," he said.

"Thank you," I said. "Are you reading my mind?"

"Alas, my scientists have not come up with a way to read minds as of yet, though our giant's blood does give us something of a connection. I'm sure there will be a way to refine it in time."

I rolled my eyes. "Is everything a quest to be conquered with you?"

"I like challenges," Ivan said. "It keeps the mind sharp. Speaking of which..." He picked up a book from one of the end tables, closing it and carefully placing it back on his shelf. "There are some challenges in the empire at the moment which are going to require us to depart the capital."

"The resistance," I said.

Ivan nodded. "I know you had contact with them, and so we've been having our informants root them out. We still haven't uncovered their base of operations, but we did discover they are going to create chaos at the palace sometime in the near future. I'm certain my automatons can handle it, but we don't want to take any risks."

"So we're going somewhere?"

Ivan turned to me. "We're going to move up the timetable of the wedding. But there's a couple of matters I'd like to discuss with you before we depart."

I blinked, not aware he had a date for the wedding in mind. "What do you mean?"

"One, I want your assurances that the Rislandians will not work with the resistance. I know you'd have told your intelligence of them, but we are not going to be able to facilitate peace between our peoples if your people work toward undermining my authority."

I swallowed, not sure what to say. I also wasn't sure I had any say over the matter—my father and Queen Reina would do what they thought was right for the kingdom. "I don't have that kind of power."

"No, but they will listen to you. Pen a missive to them urging them to make sure they work with me. I'll be sending a courier to Rislandia City regardless with the wedding invitations for whomever you choose, including your new Queen Reina."

I couldn't imagine Reina making a trip into Ivan's territory for any reason, but it seemed sensible. "I can do that. Will you pull your men from Loveridge like I've been asking?"

Ivan stared at me for a long moment. "Consider it done, as a wedding gift to you."

Again Ivan surprised me by deferring to my request on territory. Could it really be this easy to stop all of the warring? I started to think I'd made a mistake in spurning his advances on me from the beginning. But how could I have possibly trusted him then?

"Okay," I said, agreeing. It shouldn't have been this easy to agree with him. It unsettled my core. None of this seemed real. I kept thinking I would wake up from some absurd dream, but it never happened.

"Great," Ivan said. "We will be leaving for the southwestern coast past The Great Desert immediately. There is a little place, Carnait Cove, which is the most beautiful location in my entire empire—a well-kept secret I will be sharing with you."

I hadn't heard of the cove, but it didn't surprise me. Leaving for a remote location so immediately, however, set my nerves on end. I wasn't ready for this. Not yet. "Do we have to leave now?"

"It's for your safety. I have another measure to assist you on that score, since we will be traveling south by land until we reach our naval harbor." He snapped his fingers.

Dr. Metzengerstein entered, along with two lab assistants who held leather straps about as long as my arms with metal wiring in between them.

"What's this?" I asked. "Something to do with the crystals?"

"The crystals are a part of it," Ivan said, "but not in the way you'll be actively using them in the future. I mentioned my changeling net to you when we were in Rislandia City. I had Dr. Metzengerstein construct one for you."

"We'll have to work on the sizing. The field it projects has little room for error, so if you wouldn't mind holding still for us."

This device had immense military capabilities. Getting my hands on one could mean...

Not much from a remote location in the Wyranth Empire. Here I was getting some of the best information possible on the war front, and I couldn't use it. Ivan must have known that.

Still, being able to utilize this strange technology was exhilarating. I held still while Dr. Metzengerstein and his assistants placed the straps around me and tightened them.

Ivan watched. "Ideally, you'll put this on beneath your clothing so the clothing itself will be part of the field, but this is a good test. Once you know how to put it on, you'll be able to manipulate it yourself, as I do."

He flicked his hand, and his whole visage shimmered as if it were some heat mirage in the middle of the desert. When it returned, he had a beard, grey hair, and sagging eyes, making him appear much older. His suit became brown worker's clothes. I wouldn't have recognized him if I hadn't seen him transition right in front of me. "It's truly incredible technology."

"And the same crystal does this?" I asked.

Ivan shook his head. "No, this comes from the life crystal. We discovered a cache of these crystals on the Isle du Mystere."

"They power your automatons, too," I said, realizing the ability to give life must have come from something called a life crystal.

"Very astute. We have a limited supply, but it turns out a mere sliver of these crystals works miracles. The changeling net requires more than the automatons to function, which is why I have so few of these devices made."

One of the straps cut off the circulation in my arm when Dr. Metzengerstein tightened it. "Ow," I said.

"Sorry," he said, loosening the strap some. "That better?"

"Much."

Dr. Metzengerstein stepped back to survey his work. He circled me. "Looks good. Now you'll have two receptors, one on each of your palms. Depress your third and fourth fingers onto the captor and twist your hands for it to take effect. The device will interact with your brainwaves in order to shift your appearance. Only think of what you want to be—though keep the appearance similar enough to you. It glitches if you try to veer too far."

I held the receptors down, the cool metal giving me a small shock when I touched them. I sucked in a breath, and my heart beat a little faster.

One of the scientist's assistants produced a mirror and held it in front of me.

I twisted my hands, holding down on the receptors. What did I want to look like? I thought of Talyen, with her long, dark hair and slightly more pointed face with higher cheekbones than mine.

Nothing happened.

"I'm trying," I said.

"Will it," Ivan said.

I took a deep breath and solidified the image of Talyen's face in my mind. This time, the shimmering effect occurred just as it had done with Ivan. I found my face replaced with Talyen's. It was eerie having her stare back at me in the mirror. I moved my mouth from side to side, making faces, and it worked. "Whoa."

"Now release the receptors with this in place and it will stay on until you double tap on the receptors again," Dr. Metzengerstein said.

I released them. Talyen's face stayed with me. I could hardly believe it. I turned to the older gentleman who was Ivan. "This is almost as fun as flying an airship."

"It can be. Now let's write the letter to your government and get you packed," Ivan said. He turned his changeling net off, returning to his natural form. He motioned to a desk in the corner of the room. I made my way over.

I finally was doing something useful. I wished I could see the looks on the faces of my friends when they found out Loveridge would be returned to Rislandia.

CHAPTER 25

THE WIND BLEW through my hair as I stood on the deck of the *W.S.S. Adventurer*. The Wyranth preferred to name their ships after inspiring ideals rather than after people like we did in Rislandia. I pushed some of my hair back from my face, enjoying the sun, the fresh and salty air. Steam blew from the top of a large stack as gears clanked, spinning the wheels of a paddle box toward the back of the ship.

Being a military vessel, it had cannons on the top deck, aimed to the sides, the front, and back of the vessel, with a pilot house up top. The ship churned quickly through the southern waters off the Wyranth Coast, waves pelting against the shore.

Ivan came up to the railing beside me. "Are you cold?" he asked.

I tilted my head to look at him. He doted on me quite a bit, always ensuring I was fed or in comfort. It was nice of him. I could have never imagined thinking of him as a real person, but here I stood.

"No," I answered. "I like it out here. It reminds me of being on the airship." I returned my gaze to the western horizon ahead, shining waters with sunlight reflecting off of it.

"Ah, yes. Hopefully we will be able to get you into the air soon enough."

What was that supposed to mean? I had the feeling he was trying to get me to ask the question, so of course I wouldn't oblige. "You'll let me fly on Rislandia's airship once this is over?"

Ivan laughed and fidgeted with a crystal in his hand. I'd thrown the question back on him in a way he didn't anticipate. "We'll see. I'll be meeting with the captain if you need anything. The crew is at your disposal as well."

"Thanks," I said as he walked away.

We hadn't had much need of the changeling nets on the journey south—or perhaps it was because of our use of them that no one bothered us. Part of me had braced for some kind of rebellious uprising attacking our horseless carriage, much like the bandits had when I first left Rislandia, but none came.

I found myself itching for some action, but this might be as close as I would get for some time, unless Ivan asked me to try to work the crystals again. I'm sure he wanted to obtain more power through them, or he wouldn't be so focused on them.

The steamship navigated the waters by the shore, keeping a safe enough distance from the rocks, but always keeping land in sight. We passed a couple of small villages and a port, and then the land became barren, with no one along the southern shore. I understood we would pass a large desert in the western Wyranth empire, where it would have been impossible to live, but it surprised me to see such a lack of activity on the coast. This Carnait Cove he took me to would be very remote.

Eventually, I tired of watching the shoreline and decided to explore the ship. It was long, with two decks—the bottom featuring crew quarters, the top with a mess much like on the *Liliana*, and the pilot's cabin above and at the center of the ship rather than at the back.

The Wyranth soldiers greeted me as one would royalty, maintaining pleasant attitudes and smiles every time I came across one of them. It would take me a while to get used to the deference, as I expected a more hostile reaction.

Automaton guards stood every dozen or so feet along the deck, creating a looming sense of oppression despite the open air.

I decided to retire to my quarters and take a nap while waiting for the ship to finish its course.

In the late evening I became stir crazy. My body wanted to be on the move, not lying in a bed—a combination of excitement and fear made me jittery.

In a few days, I would be married at a pompous ceremony in the cove. It wasn't just a theory anymore. This would be a permanent, life-altering event.

I wasn't ready. How could I be? Every fiber of my being wanted to run to the rails of the ship, jump off, and swim away as far as I could. But that would be foolish. I couldn't do it. For one, I had no idea of the geography in which we traveled. Second, it would mean all the sacrifices I'd already made had been in vain. I made this decision to help Rislandia, and despite my instincts, I had to follow through with it.

Maybe I could talk to Ivan. He had a calming manner about him, even though he could be infuriatingly arrogant. Would he still be awake?

I got up from the small bed in my cabin and strapped on my belt with my pistol holster attached—another surprise in Ivan allowing me to keep a weapon. Come to think of it, Ivan had allowed everything I'd requested. When I'd needed to go see Rislandian troops, he'd allowed it. He'd also let me return to Rislandia City when I wanted to see my people. He hadn't been the over-bearing monster I'd been expecting at all.

Everything had changed. I couldn't think of him as a monster any longer. The Wyranth had killed so many of my people, caused so much grief, but it went to show that once you got to know a person, there was often more to them than what you had in your mind. I wished everyone could see beyond the surface and the disagreements to come to that conclusion. What a better world we'd live in.

I might have discovered the key to world peace, but I still couldn't sleep.

The moon shone down on water, gentle waves hitting the ship in the darkness of night. The corridors of the ship had shadows cast about them, but with enough of a glow from the stars outside and light seeping in that it allowed me to see my way. Now if only I could remember where Ivan slept.

The corridors all looked the same, but I finally reached an area where I had left Ivan earlier. A figure moved in front of the door, opening it slowly.

"Ivan?" I asked in a whisper.

The figure froze, a man concealed by shadows. I wished I could see better but we were closer to the center of the ship where no light from the outside reached us. He didn't respond but he turned toward me. Something shimmered in his hand, metallic.

With the man facing fully toward me, I could tell it wasn't Ivan. He didn't have the same lanky figure, but was a little stockier, broader around the shoulders. This man was trying to sneak into Ivan's quarters.

He rushed me.

The metallic glint in his hand caught the light from the hallway—a knife arced through the air. I ducked. My attacker's miss caused him to stumble forward. I took the opportunity to push myself ahead, jamming my shoulder into his belly.

He hadn't expected such resistance, and slammed against the corridor wall before losing his footing and falling to the floor. On his descent, he slashed his knife upward, clipping the edge of my blouse and cutting a hole at my stomach, but he missed my flesh.

I backpedaled. "Help! Guards!" I shouted, not sure if there was anyone within earshot.

Then, I remembered my pistol.

It should have been my first instinct to go for the gun, but even though I'd done some training drills with my crew, I hadn't been in too many direct combat situations. Most of the times I had ended up engaged in battle resulted in me running or being rescued by my ferret.

My heart raced and my breath quickened. The man scrambled to get to his feet. I had to act decisively.

I reached to my holster and produced my pistol. "Hold it," I said, trying to get him not to move.

Ivan's door flung open.

The Iron Emperor walked into the scene, silhouetted by the light from his room, looking on in horror. Blood drained from his face. He wore night clothes, silken baby-blue attire with big buttons on the front. It looked very comfortable, but not good for battle. "What's going on here? I'm trying to sl—"

The man struck at Ivan with his knife.

Sweat moistened my hands. I don't know what made me so nervous. When I tried to pull the trigger, my fingers nearly slipped, but I managed anyway. The pistol resounded with a bang which made me jump back.

The assassin dropped the knife on the floor. It clanged. He gripped his chest with his hand and fell slack on the floor.

Ivan stood with his mouth agape, but soon returned to his stoic, unreadable countenance. As he composed himself, multiple Wyranth soldiers entered the corridor. They brandished their guns—and pointed them at me!

I dropped my pistol and put my hands up. "Don't shoot!" I said.

"Seize the Rislandian!" one of the Wyranth soldiers said.

Someone grabbed my hands from behind and pulled them behind my back hard. Whoever had done so nearly ripped my arms from their sockets. I winced.

"Release her," Ivan said in a low, commanding tone.

The Wyranth complied. I turned to see the man who grabbed me, a gruff man in uniform, complete with his pointed helmet. I wanted to slap him, but instead I rubbed my shoulders. By Malaky, that hurt.

Ivan glanced at his attacker, narrowing his eyes. Did he recognize the man? He crouched to the ground. "He's still breathing," Ivan said. "Take him to the brig and prepare him for interrogation."

"Do you know who he is?" I asked.

Ivan shook his head. "He must be a member of the resistance. I can't see the Rislandians sending an assassin at this point. We'll find out who sent him and take care of it." His voice held a dark and calculating coolness. One might have thought there hadn't been an attempt on his life a moment earlier. He stood and took my hand. "Are you all right?"

I took a moment to breathe. The whole situation had happened so fast I'd hardly had time to process it. I'd shot a man. It'd been awhile since I'd done something like that. I'd fired bullets in the war, of course, but I'd seen very little violence in recent months.

The Wyranth took the assassin away. He wasn't going to die, though I didn't want to think about what the Wyranth did to would-be assassins of their emperor in an interrogation session.

I took a deep breath in and out to calm myself. "Yeah, I'm fine. I'm just glad I got here when I did. He almost snuck into your room."

Ivan shook his head. "Perhaps I should post a guard inside as well." He motioned to one of his men as if it were an order, and the Wyranth soldier stepped past Ivan and into the room. Ivan squeezed my hand. "I'm grateful. You saved my life. I owe you. What are you doing around here anyway?"

I bit my lip. "I couldn't sleep. Wanted to talk. Guess it was a silly thought, with you asleep."

"It's your luck," Ivan said, pointing to his skull. "Giant's cognitive intuition. The blood must be stronger in you than I thought. Amazing." He released my hand. "I'll post a guard on you, just in case. I doubt there's others on board, though. You should be safe. We couldn't have that many defectors."

"Thanks," I said.

"Try to get some sleep. It's going to be busy from here on out until the wedding."

I walked away feeling no more fulfilled than I had been to start. The evening had gone by so fast. Could Ivan be right about my blood giving me some strange premonitions? My intuition had always been good. A year ago, I would have told him he was crazy. Now I couldn't be so sure.

CHAPTER 26

THE STEAMSHIP PULLED into a harbor, which had long docks designed to guide sea traffic into the cove—a peninsula of land extending outward to hold back the waves of the Golgmarsh Ocean. Calm waters made it easy to guide the ship into the bay, where four more such naval vessels were docked, along with several other smaller ships.

A long wall rose along the shore beyond the harbor, comprised of elegant light stone, raised slightly above a walkway beyond where some of the cove's inhabitants stood watching the seaward traffic. To the south the blues of open ocean stretched as far as I could see. A blustery wind blew, bringing a chill from the Southwest, but it calmed as we reached our dock.

The crew extended a bridge across from the ship to land and assisted me onto it. Servants and guards came with our bags behind us.

Ivan strode across the bridge as if he owned the place—which I suppose as emperor he did—and greeted some of the local dockworkers with handshakes. He said hellos and listened to them, operating in a political capacity I hadn't seen him in before.

I supposed to retain an empire he would have to communicate with his people, but in our interactions, he'd always seemed so reclusive.

Just another oddity along this journey. How many more would I see?

I followed Ivan but stayed quiet unless he introduced me. Unlike the Wyranth capital, which had its tension from the brewing resistance, the locals here appeared to like their emperor. They paid little heed to the automatons crossing the bridge behind us, clacking slowly across the bridge in great numbers. How many of those abominations did Ivan bring with us?

We made our way to large steps which spiraled up onto the wall, revealing a platform beyond with some houses, an inn, and a larger residence. Twin towers marked the end of each of the walls, one monitoring the west, and one the south.

In all, Carnait Cove was more a quaint town, like a Loveridge, rather than a larger city like Portsgate or Rislandia City. The naval stations looked to be a new addition, as beyond the water lay nothing but a smattering of trees along grassy fields and rolling plains. The spaciousness almost felt like home.

Ivan showed me around the town, introducing me to his local governor, Baldwin, who managed the southwestern coast of the Wyranth Empire. Baldwin was a pleasant, middle-aged man with a receding hairline—it took everything in me to refrain from making a joke about his name—and a hearty belly laugh. He brought levity to what was already a peaceful place, putting me more at ease.

We wasted no time, as Ivan took me to a small park on the coast, with fresh-cut grass, rose bushes lining each side, and a small wooden awning out near the water. The awning brought shade, but was open, allowing a view of the sea. Servants took measurements of the area.

"This is where we will be wed," Ivan said. "I've given a week's time, which I should hope is ample notice for any Rislandians who wish to attend to make it here by steamboat. I've granted leave to cross the empire, so there should be no trouble with their safety—assuming the resistance leaves them alone."

I held my tongue at the assumption. The resistance wanted our help. They wouldn't attack Rislandians. But I surveyed the area and tried to ignore the politics of the situation.

It would have been the perfect place for a wedding if I'd actually desired to get married. That was the problem with this scenario, wasn't it? I glanced out the corner of my eye to Ivan, who had already gone to interact with some of the other servants, pointing and directing them. By all rights, he was a good-looking man. A girl could do worse, and as emperor, he certainly had the means to provide. I still would have given my right arm to be marrying Ethan in this lovely scenery, not him. That path was closed to me now, though, and it had been my choice. I had to be content with what I had.

In many ways, being around Ivan had given me a new appreciation for him. I cared for him to some degree. At least I understood him as a real person, and not some devilish figurehead enemy. If only I could sit him down with Queen Reina and my father and work something out between all of us. There had to be a way for everyone to live peacefully.

It wasn't my people who would refuse the peace though. Ivan's ambitions maintained our conflict. I understood the need for land to feed his people, but surely with the way his people could invent war machines as they had—not to mention the automatons— we could reach a mutually-agreeable arrangement. I could only imagine what an abundance we could have if the Wyranth scientific minds put their ingenuity toward farming instead of weapons of war.

It might have all been wishful thinking, but it was the basis for what I'd work toward as Empress of the Wyranth. I blinked. Empress. I couldn't believe I thought of myself with such a title. Even "baron" had been such a shock for a young farm girl with little to her name. How easy I'd gotten swept up into nobility and the world of politics. It reminded me of when Ethan commented how we were the only eligible nobility aboard the *Liliana* together...

No. I had to stop thinking about Ethan. I shook my head.

"Is something the matter?" Ivan asked, returning to me. "It is warm out. Would you like my servants to fetch you some water?"

"No, just jitters," I said.

Ivan appraised me. For a moment, I thought he might offer to rescind the proposal, but that may have been another fantasy of mine. "It's natural to be afraid of change, but change is also the natural human condition. Nothing can stay the same, and yet what does remain constant is the cycles in life. Difficult times, good times, they can be counted on to continue in waves." He motioned to the sea. "Much like the ocean crashing against the shore."

"You aren't afraid of marrying some strange girl from Rislandia?" I half-smiled, trying to lighten my mood.

Ivan chuckled. "It's been my plan since learning you'd been captured in my territory the first time."

"True," I said.

Ivan turned to the water, his cool eyes losing focus in the distance. "No, I don't fear my choice. It's the best political move I could make, given the tenuous situation with my neighboring kingdom. And you know the other reasons of your genetic line."

"I'd always hoped to marry because of my care for the other person," I said, prodding in hopes he might share similar sentiments. Sometimes he displayed humanity, other times he was so cold and calculating it made me feel like an object to him. All my goodwill from a moment prior had evaporated. I gripped the fabric of my skirt to keep myself from socking him.

"That comes with time," Ivan said. "Spending time around someone, you can't help but feel attachment. Making decisions of an entire life, future heirs to an empire, based on some fleeting lust?" Ivan shook his head. "That is the problem with modern society. It's amazing the human race is propagating with such foolish ideas."

"Love isn't foolish," I said.

Ivan turned to me, quirking a brow. "Is it not? What good does it do?"

"I'm here because I *love* my country. My love is going to save thousands of lives."

"Ah, idealism," Ivan said. "Understandable. Though from my perspective, the world is much darker than you believe. I take steps to mitigate potential failures or loss of power."

"I know," I said, crossing my arms. "It's maddening."

Ivan laughed again.

"It's not funny."

"It is. I admit, I like your spunkiness and your commitment to your ideals. It exudes strength I haven't found in many women, let alone the noble prospects my advisors would have foisted on me."

Here he was, opening up and being human again. In his own way, it was an admission that he liked me better than anyone else. I relaxed a little, though the words also made my insides flutter. Why did I care about his approval? Maybe it was spending more time with him as he had said. My heart grew fonder in his presence for certain, but then, I had similar experiences with the absence of some people—namely Ethan. I wished I could control my feelings and not be so up and down.

It was my nerves. This wedding came all too quickly. I tried to breathe in the fresh air and calm myself. "What good are my genetics to you anyway? The crystals, the giant's blood, to what end?"

Ivan scanned my eyes as if searching me. "You will judge me poorly if I say more."

"You can't be honest with me?"

"Not yet," Ivan said. "In time you'll grow to understand the renaissance I aim to bring about for the world."

What was that supposed to mean? It drove me mad when he spoke like this. "If I'm to be empress, I should know."

"You'll know. When you're empress." Ivan held firm. He stepped forward toward me.

My foot instinctively moved backward, but I held my ground. If this was another test...

Ivan leaned over and pressed his lips to mine. A soft kiss, nothing passionate, nothing tawdry, but one of affection all the same.

Stunned, I didn't move until he pulled back again, eyes wide at his bright blue eyes staring at mine. His lips were softer than I would have expected, pleasantly so. I touched my fingers to my own, disbelieving what had just occurred.

"Another matter to get used to," Ivan said, giving me a sheepish smile. "Here's something I will confess. That was my first."

I blinked. "I don't believe you."

"I never lie," Ivan said. "Come now. Let's move onto more pleasant things," he said, taking me by the hand and turning me away from the wedding location. "You'll be meeting my personal seamstress, who handles both my suits and Kristina's attire. She is an incredible woman who's been crafting our clothing since birth. I believe she's nearly finished with your dress and just needs to alter it to the proper sizing."

A dress? For me? Of course, there would be. I hurried to keep pace with Ivan's long legs as he led me toward the inn. Even though Ivan had explained his reasonings to me, it still didn't make sense. Everything since receiving the offer of marriage in exchange for the airship plans in Rislandia City had come like a whirlwind. Still, with so much attention being showered on me, it was a lot better than all the fighting I'd done in the months prior.

Even though I couldn't get comfortable with the wedding, my relationship with Ivan had been better than expected. I had to be missing something important about these crystals or Ivan's future plans that would ruin this all. It would come, I could feel it. Something had to give.

CHAPTER 27

IVAN TOOK THE next three days to build a makeshift office out of the local inn, appropriating one of their tables as a desk, where his books, maps, and war plans were all set. He also had construction plans for bridges along the Border River. Perhaps Rislandia would permanently lose land in this conflict, but such bridges and infrastructure could only be good for the people of the south in the long run. He didn't hide the plans from me, but rather explained them along with the benefits it would have. After listening to him, I found I agreed with his vision for the immediate future, which unsettled my stomach, but anything beat an endless war between our two countries.

The way he explained things to me, he wanted to prepare me to be a partner for him in these matters. I wanted to try to help, give advice, but I figured now wouldn't be the time to do so. I had plenty of time to assert myself later when I had more authority. I'd been used to paper-pushing and having not much to do over the last several months, and hopefully with this wedding, I'd have much more to do. At least Ivan kept me informed on what was going on in the world.

As promised, Ivan had his troops pulled back from Loveridge. The new line was to the south, and Rislandia had its town again. If I accomplished nothing else, I'd managed to do this for my kingdom. I hoped Queen Reina and the others appreciated it, though I felt selfish for wanting the acknowledgement.

Word of a ceasefire already began to trickle through to the other contested regions of the border, making it easier for Ivan to focus on the internal issues with his kingdom. He granted various soldiers lordships and property rights for their service. One sheet on his desk read Project Mecha, piquing my curiosity since he didn't show it to me. Perhaps with some luck, I'd be able to rifle through and find information for back home.

Should I even think of Rislandia as back home anymore? Despite not giving me all of the information, Ivan clued me in on enough of what was going on that it felt like he trusted me. It would be difficult, if not impossible, to start thinking of myself as Empress of the Wyranth. I wondered how Reina or my father would be able to conceive of me as royalty.

A Wyranth soldier entered, an older man with a shrewd-looking face, sharply pointed chin which almost seemed a mirror to his helmet. Medals adorned his uniform. He stopped and saluted.

"At ease, General Gregor," Ivan said, looking up at him and giving a half-hearted salute.

General Gregor dropped his salute and let his hand fall stiffly to his side. "Thank you, sir."

"What brings you here? You look out of sorts," Ivan said.

I glanced at the general, unable to discern anything but a tense seriousness to him.

"Yes, sir," General Gregor said. "There is an armed encampment which popped up beyond the city walls overnight, and they are drawing closer."

Ivan raised a brow. "Rislandians?"

"No, sir. It appears to be the resistance."

Ivan stared at his maps for a long moment, sighed, and then drew his hands together to crack his knuckles. "They must be foolish to try to raise an insurrection out in the open," he said, the wheels spinning in his head. He wrinkled his brow. "No, a gamble. They hope the residents of the cove will see their example and join their usurping me. We can't allow that to happen."

General Gregor kept his lips tight, allowing Ivan to talk.

Ivan glanced at me. "I don't relish using force on my people, but an open rebellion gives me little choice."

I'm not sure why he explained himself to me, but I wanted to curl up into a ball. I didn't want to be a participant in ordering conflict between Ivan's forces and those rebels who sought my help. "General," Ivan said, turning his attention to the man, "dispatch units one and four of the automaton brigade to handle them."

"Yes, sir," General Gregor said, saluting again. He spun on his feet and exited the room.

Ivan stood, clasping his hands together, and then slipped out from behind his desk to follow General Gregor.

"Where are you going?" I asked.

"To survey the battle. This will be an interesting test of my new brigade's effectiveness," he said. "Join me." He motioned for me to follow.

I didn't want to go with him. The last thing I wanted to watch was robots battling poorly trained civilians. Ivan hadn't even tried diplomacy with them, but I didn't feel comfortable telling him what to do about his own people. If it had been Rislandians out there...

...I would have been scratching and kicking at Ivan to try to make him stop.

But these weren't Rislandians.

We departed the inn, the humid warm air of the cove thick on my face, causing me to sweat. Ivan headed to one of the watchtowers along the coast. His guard followed the two of us, and we made our way up spiraled stairs along the tower, until we reached the platform at the top.

Two soldiers stood on the tower already, holding their rifles trained on the small specks inland, which appeared to be the encampment. The soldiers wore goggles that made their eyes look exceedingly large. They must have acted like spyglasses or binoculars.

"Don't fire yet," Ivan said to the snipers. "I don't want to give them any time to prepare. This will be an interesting test. Might I borrow one of your goggles?"

The soldier ripped the goggles from his face, which left a dented impression in his skin, and handed them to Ivan.

"Ah, Zaira, would you like a pair?" Ivan asked.

"Not particularly," I said. If I narrowed my eyes, I could see well enough. I didn't need a close up view of what was sure to be a gory battle.

Ivan slipped the goggles over his face and tightened the strap as he turned his attention to the encampment. "Fifty of them. What are they thinking? They know that's not a sizable enough of a force to be able to..."

His eyes went wide. "They want to be martyrs." Ivan turned to the soldier he'd just stolen the goggles from. "Find General Gregor. Give him orders to have our automatons capture and disarm—not kill. Quickly."

"Yes, sir," the soldier said before hustling down the stairs.

"Ah, Zaira. This could have been disastrous. They intended on getting massacred, and then spreading a disinformation campaign about it back home. We'll have to stave this off. Though I'm not sure where we can comfortably keep them as prisoners here," Ivan said, surveying the small town around us. "There will be too many guests present."

"Put them on one of the ships," I said.

"Ah, good idea." Ivan grinned. "It's useful having you around." He gazed out past the town's walls once more. "I hope we're not too late in relaying orders."

I narrowed my eyes to get a better glimpse of the area outside the walls. I could see where the automatons moved to meet with the resistance fighters, even if I couldn't get great detail. It was better this way. I'd seen battles up close through the gyromatic telescope on the *Liliana*, and some views aren't meant to be seen close up.

The two forces clashed. Gunshots rang out, echoing as far as here. It was impossible to say what kind of force the automatons used. Ivan stared intently through his magnifying goggles, expressionless as usual. I wished I could read him a little better.

Maybe I could if I tried. Didn't the giants have some sort of telepathic ability, one in which they fed on emotions? I tried to feel Ivan, for lack of a better term. It might have just been a foolish thought, but if I did have giant blood in my system, who knew what I was capable of?

Nothing happened.

I laughed.

"Something amusing?" Ivan asked without sparing a glance for me.

I turned back to the battle. "Just laughing at myself."

"Ah," Ivan said. "The battle goes well. It looks as if General Gregor received my message in time. The automatons have broken a few bones of those who fought, but nothing more. No casualties so far, at least by our forces. And the resistance doesn't appear to know how to fight the automatons either. They're firing guns helplessly at them."

I looked out toward the battle once more. Without my own goggles, I could only get impressions, more difficult as dust and debris kicked up from the action, but it appeared the resistance were being driven back away from the city. Automatons incapacitated some, leaving them where they fell. But if Ivan was right, those fighters were just injured, not dead.

"Good, a few will be captured. We'll need information about their leaders and where their base of operations is. Time to nip this in the bud," Ivan said.

JON DEL ARROZ

The battle continued, with the resistance backing further and further away from the city as the automatons advanced. They had no chance. Ivan must have been right about them wanting to be martyrs. I couldn't imagine going into battle with the intention of losing. It wasn't the von Monocle way. But I understood the idea—show how vicious of a tyrant Ivan was. The only problem was... Ivan wasn't as bad as everyone made him out to be. His reputation had a calculated tactical purpose, as with everything else he did.

The automatons nearly drove the resistance fighters away, but then more forms appeared over the horizon. They came closer. Reinforcements? I pointed toward them. "Ivan, what are those? Are there more of your troops coming?"

Ivan frowned. "No, I'm not sure where they're coming from."

A projectile landed right in the middle of the automaton forces. It exploded with a force incomparable in the battle so far. Several automatons went flying, blasted into parts. Dirt rose into the air from where the projectile had hit. Were the resistance fighters we saw a first wave, luring Ivan's troops out into the field of battle? How many went out there? I wondered if we'd been left defenseless.

I tensed, suddenly in fear for my life. What if the resistance managed to capture Carnait Cove? They wouldn't have any qualms assassinating Ivan, but what about me? I couldn't imagine I'd be spared from their wrath, especially as I hadn't come through with any aid for them.

Now the automatons retreated. Another projectile flew, tearing into the ranks of Ivan's mechanical men. If these were real people, it would have been a bloody sight to witness. I still couldn't get a good view through the haze in the air. They were too far off. Did the resistance have artillery in their second line that Ivan hadn't accounted for?

But the fighters who first approached the city didn't seem to want to continue their efforts. They scattered, running away as if trying to get clear of the two competing forces. I couldn't help it anymore and wanted to get a closer look. "Can I use the goggles?" I asked.

Ivan was fixated on the battle. Instead of his stoic look, he appeared genuinely worried. "Those are supposed to be my units," Ivan said.

"What units? Let me see."

He took the goggles off and offered them to me. "How could the resistance have gotten ahold of them? This isn't right!"

I pressed the goggles to my face, not wanting to waste time strapping them over my head.

The battle became much clearer as I saw all of the automatons in detail, along with the resistance men running haphazardly, their line broken. Beyond them was something I'd never seen before.

Two bulbous contraptions loomed over everything, as big as five men with metal arms and legs on their joints. They fired projectiles as they stepped forward awkwardly, mechanical in motion rather than the fluid movements of men. The center bulbs were large pods with tubes and wires protruding from them and two smokestacks out the back, angled toward their rear, producing smoke. One arm had a projectile launcher, with the ammunition inside the arm, while the other sprayed flames.

These two devices wreaked havoc on everything around them. "By Malaky, what am I looking at?"

"Those," Ivan said, "are *Project Mecha.*"

I now understood the classified documents I'd wanted to see earlier. But why weren't they fighting for Ivan? Had the resistance captured Ivan's new military toys?

Smoke clouded the scenery, but as they pressed forward to the town, people came into view behind the giant mecha units. Soldiers lined the front of the group, advancing with much more discipline than the resistance displayed.

My breath stilled as I spotted a familiar crimson color to the flags they carried. These weren't resistance fighters.

They were Rislandians.

CHAPTER 28

I HAD ALREADY run halfway down the watchtower by the time Ivan caught up with me. He grabbed me by the arm with a force I hadn't felt from him prior. I nearly fell in surprise.

"What do you think you're doing?" Ivan asked.

"I'm going to warn my people. You tell your general to stop the automatons from attacking them."

"There are bullets flying out there," Ivan said.

"I know. That's why I've got to go now."

He stared at me, frowning. "We should send a messenger. You're too important to risk."

"If they see me, they might stop the fighting sooner. I'm your best hope." I couldn't let any bloodshed happen. There were Rislandian lives on the line. If even one died, it would be too many.

Ivan let go of my arm. "Your plan is foolhardy. I hope you'll remember how much leeway and freedom I've given you. It's been intentional," he said.

I nodded. "I know. And I appreciate it. Trust me. I'll be okay. They won't hurt me."

"You'll have your luck with you," Ivan said. He proceeded down the steps. "I'll find General Gregor. Hopefully, we will be able to stop the automatons by the time you get out to the field."

I didn't want to wait for him to change his mind. I ran down the steps and toward the battlefield, heading through the gates of the small settlement. Guards watched me with puzzled expressions as I passed. I moved as fast as I could, the wind blowing my hair into my face.

The smoke and dust were much thicker on the battlefield than it appeared from up in the tower. My breaths burned from inhaling some of the soot, but I didn't dare slow my pace. Each moment could mean a Rislandian life.

I reached the battle within minutes. The resistance fighters had fled, the automatons turning their attentions to the Rislandians, who retreated behind the large mecha units. One of the mechas shot flames from its arm socket, melting an automaton near me. I could feel the heat even from behind them.

Rislandian bullets flew in my direction, most of them pinging off of automatons. I was still far enough back to not be safe from the crossfire, but I had to find a way to advance forward and not have them target me.

I looped around the tall grasses to the side of the battle, trying to give myself a wide berth, so I could be easily seen, and not be mistaken for one of the automatons.

One of the automatons engaged with one of the mecha units, banging its metallic arm into the chest cavity of the mecha. It dented the mecha unit, but the mecha used its arm to swipe across and send the automaton flying. The Wyranth creature crashed not too far from me, causing me to jump backward and yelp. If it had been thrown just a few feet further...

But I couldn't worry about what might have been. I was still alive. I could stop this battle.

Another round of gunshots rang out. I was still too close to the battle.

I dropped to the ground, narrowly avoiding bullets whizzing past where I'd stood. My heart pounded in my chest, adrenaline giving me a surge of energy, but the shock of the moment froze me, with my face planted in the grass. Within a span of moments, I'd been so close to being killed twice. I could have lost everything.

Maybe Ivan was right. I rushed into this without really planning. But would it have been better to send some unsuspecting Wyranth into this mess?

I didn't value myself above another the way Ivan seemed to put me on a pedestal because of my genetics. All I could do was keep pressing forward. And I had to do it before one of these stray bullets clipped me.

I crawled forward on my hands and legs, the tall grasses and weeds scraping against my skin and my clothes. It'd leave marks for sure, and I already itched. It didn't matter though, I had to keep going.

Inch by inch, I pushed myself forward. My arms burned from the strain, as I wasn't used to moving like this. It gave me an appreciation for the infantry soldiers, who had to crawl across the ground with large packs on their backs regularly. It must have been difficult.

I scraped my knees on pebbles which weren't visible through the grasses. The pain seared through me, but I pressed forward. The *whirring* of the power cores of the automatons stopped. They froze in place, though the Rislandians still fired.

It took a few more feet of crawling to get out of their immediate targeting range. I stood slowly, putting my hands up. This was the most dangerous part, and I hoped by Malaky my people wouldn't shoot on sight. "Cease fire!" I shouted for good measure.

The soldiers behind the mecha units took notice of me first. They pointed guns at me. I tensed. This would be my moment of truth.

"Hold!" one of the soldiers shouted. "It's just a girl."

I stepped forward to make sure my words carried better to the soldiers. "The automatons have been called off. They're not here to fight you. The people they were engaged with were Wyranth resistance attacking the settlement."

"Good we helped them, then," one of the soldiers said. Others muttered agreement.

"Good or not," I said, trying to be diplomatic, "it's not our fight."

"Our?" the first soldier asked.

I trudged toward them further so they could get a better look at me. "That's right," I said. "I'm Zaira von Monocle. I came out so you wouldn't get hurt in a needless skirmish."

The mecha had stopped moving during the conversation, and I could hear them power down. No more exhaust came from them. "Zaira?" A muffled male voice came from inside the contraption. The bulbous core of it shook, and a plate cracked open.

CHAPTER 29

THE FRONT HATCH of the mecha unit popped open. Inside, drenched in sweat and worn, Ethan von Lantern smiled at me. He jiggled the latch to a harness holding him in place, and fell from the unit, crouching as he landed on the dirt.

Even as unkempt as he was, my heart fluttered at the sight of him. I ran forward as he made it to his feet and embraced him. "Ethan! I've missed you so much."

The Wyranth automatons retreated back into Carnait Cove. There was no sign of any of the resistance fighters anywhere near us. They must have fled when the two strange mechanical forces met.

Ethan squeezed me. "Me too," he said in a low, somber voice. He pulled back to look at me, the excitement disappearing from his eyes. "What, by Malaky, have you done while I was gone?"

I opened my mouth to answer, but the plating on the other mecha unit popped open, James jumping out from it. "It's uncomfortable in those things, but so incredible! Ethan, did you see the way I used the flamethrower to melt that Wyranth creature?" He made a motion with his arm and a motoring noise with his lips.

Both Ethan and I looked at him incredulously.

"What?" James asked, blinking.

"Haven't you learned any tact during your time as a knight?" Ethan asked.

James shrugged. "Who needs tact when you have giant armor?"

The mecha armor still loomed over us, casting a long shadow. I frowned at the large units. "How did you get those things anyway?"

"It's a long story," Ethan said.

"We stole 'em," James said.

Ethan sighed.

I couldn't help but laugh. At least they were in good spirits— and alive. I'd been worried about their mission off to the foreign country. But beneath Ethan's levity was a sorrow he'd never had before. A sorrow for which I was at fault.

It made my stomach churn. But I didn't want to hash all of this out in front of James.

Rislandian infantrymen stood north of us, and beyond them, smokestacks from horseless carriages blasted exhaust into the air. I couldn't see who was there. "Who's with you?"

"The whole royal contingent for your wedding," James said.

Ethan's eyes narrowed.

"Why don't you go back and let them know everything's okay?" I asked.

"I'm sure they can see from where they are," James said, waving to one of the infantrymen, who waved back at him.

"Now, James," I said more firmly.

"Okay, okay." He bounded toward the others, leaving Ethan and me without anyone in earshot.

A moment passed between us, wind blowing on the grasses of the plain, softly rattling the leaves. The sound of automatons moving in the distance made the scene less desirable.

"How could you agree to marry *him?*" Ethan asked, throwing his hands back.

"I'm sorry," was all I could manage to say. He had to understand. Wouldn't he have done the same in my place?

"You should have waited for me," Ethan said.

"You know I couldn't do that. Someone had to stop the war," I said.

"It's a job for our diplomats!"

"One they'd failed at doing." I crossed my arms over my chest. "This was the best way to ensure Rislandia had its defenses restored, and to be able to enact real change. You must have heard what I've already done within the Wyranth Empire so far. They've retreated from Loveridge."

"They would have anyway with James and me in the mecha units," Ethan said.

I didn't want to argue the specific points on Wyranth and Rislandian policy. It was conjecture that Ethan and James would have been able to drive them back. What I'd done was tangible and good for Rislandia as a whole, even if it hurt like someone had torn my heart right out of my chest. I could tell Ethan felt the same way, but what good would it do to keep jabbing at his wound?

Ethan clenched his fist and closed his eyes. "I can't believe it. Everything was going so right for a change."

I bit my lip. What could I say to make it better? I couldn't undo what I'd committed to. He certainly made me feel all the guiltier for my choice.

He turned toward Carnait Cove. "I'll challenge him to a duel."

"You'll what?" My jaw dropped.

"We'll draw swords, just like the old days. It's a matter of honor."

"You're not going to duel the Iron Emperor, Ethan. I'm not enslaved by him," I said.

"You love him?" His eyes met mine.

I couldn't help but look away from him. "No, of course not."

"Then call it off."

"I gave my word, Ethan."

Silence fell between us again. It hurt so badly. I wanted to cry, but I couldn't. What an embarrassing scene that would be. It was already bad enough standing here and arguing with Ethan where the infantrymen could see our body language.

Ethan slammed his fist into his leg. "I hate this so much. I wish I'd never gone to Nyanzi. I'd have found some other way."

I doubted his presence would have changed anything except for us arguing back in Rislandia City instead of here. But maybe he would have felt less betrayed if I had talked it out with him instead of deciding while he was away. "I wish things could be different too."

He slumped his shoulders. "I get it," he said. "You're making your sacrifice. I know what the kingdom's gaining. It's just not fair!"

"No, it's not," I said, glancing at him out the corner of my eye.

Even with sweat drying on him, his hair sticking out at strange angles from being in the mecha suit, he was a handsome man. Strong arms, a serious face with a tight jaw. A dream boy. I couldn't help but compare him to Ivan, who, while having his own charms, didn't have as much of a manly spark.

I wished I could change things. "I should get back to the city and let them know I'm all right, and to have them prepare for your arrival. We can talk later."

"Yeah," Ethan said. He turned his back on me without a hug, without even one more glance. It was over between us. It'd come to reality even though I'd avoided thinking about it for the whole time he was gone.

I turned and made my way back to the wall. Away from curious eyes, tears streaked down my face.

CHAPTER 30

THE NEXT FEW days dragged on. All I wanted was to get this wedding behind me.

Most of the Rislandians made camp outside the small cove, but Queen Reina and her retinue received their own quarters in the inn. The Wyranth soldiers had an uncomfortable air to them with the large mecha parked outside, but Ivan ignored their existence for the time being.

Even though Ivan gave me ample time to spend with the Rislandians, it was awkward. Queen Reina and her advisors no longer treated me like I was one of their ranks, but like an outsider. I tried to brief her, The High Knight, and my father on everything I'd seen. They listened and thanked me, but it still felt wrong to be around them.

It was better when I was with my father. We shared every meal. I appreciated being able to spend time with him, to be together, but even so, I could sense the disappointment radiating from him. I gave up everything do what was best for my people, and it felt rotten.

After dinner one evening, my father's eyes softened as he glanced at me. "I'm sorry, Zaira. These last weeks have been difficult for me with the death of my best friend, and in essence, losing my daughter to that tyrant. I know you're doing everything you can for Rislandia, and it's something admirable, not scornworthy. But it's difficult on a father. You have to understand."

"I do," I said, finding myself tearing up again like I had multiple times since the Rislandians arrived. "I want you to be proud of me."

"I am," my father said, taking my hand from across the table and squeezing it. "I don't know that I'd be able to make the decision you had if our situations were reversed. And you've already done incredible good. Your mere presence is changing the Wyranth Empire, which of course it would." He shook his head and laughed. "Malaky knew it. He told me as soon as you entered the city, it would be like a switch turning on a motor. I doubted anyone could change the Iron Emperor, but here we are."

"I'm trying."

My father nodded. "You are. And I want more. I want reparations for the terrible things he's done to our country, but the truth is, even though he doesn't occupy Rislandia City, he won the war. We were on our last legs, and with no airship...". He shook his head again. "Yes, you did the right thing."

My shoulders relaxed. A huge burden lifted from me. As childish as it seemed, all I wanted was for someone close to me to acknowledge the good I was doing. It vindicated me—for the most part. If only Ethan could see it.

We turned the conversation to the past, to my mother, the times my father had come home and been with the three of us. Those were the most joyous times of my life, even greater than when I'd flown on the airship. I cherished those days and wanted them back just as badly. But they wouldn't come. Everything had to change. I'd get used to my new life. In some ways, I already had.

After my father finished the last glass of wine from the carafe, we parted to head for bed. The stars shone on Carnait Cove, without the street lights of a major city anywhere in sight. It was like the sky was a milky white rather than dark. I stared up at them for a long time as I walked back to Ivan's residence.

Someone grabbed my wrist, snapping me out of my reverie. I nearly jumped out of my skin, heart racing before I saw the person standing near me.

Ivan.

He didn't grab me hard. It was a gentle touch. But I hadn't been prepared for it. Plus, I was still jumpy from dodging bullets in days prior.

"Did you have a good dinner with your father?" he asked, releasing me.

"You scared me," I said, bringing my hand to my chest. My heart pounded, and not in a good way.

"My apologies. I should have alerted you to my presence."

I cocked my head at him. His beautiful blue eyes twinkled at me in the starlight.

"I am impressed with your dedication and bravery," Ivan said. "It's been a joy getting to know you over these last days. I understand why your family is so feared by my people. I hope in time your name will be revered in the same way."

"Thank you," I said in a near whisper. I wasn't sure what else I should say to such an intense declaration. It made me uncomfortable.

"I'm under no illusion that you are here for any purpose other than duty. Though I hope you've found I'm not the monster you thought I was."

"You're not."

Ivan nodded. He motioned for me to walk with him and moved at a slow pace ahead. I followed by his side in the cool evening air.

"I've spent some time meeting with your queen in person. She and I had never talked face to face," Ivan said.

"Oh?" I couldn't imagine Reina meeting with him. But I supposed we all had to do things we would rather not.

175

"She agrees it's time to end hostilities between our countries, though she's stuck on demanding the southern lands we acquired returned to Rislandia. I'm afraid there's no way we can oblige. We need tillable land."

"So many lives for land," I said, shaking my head. "Why wouldn't you just trade with us?"

"I ran the calculations. It wouldn't have worked. Rislandia would have had to give us the food, or we would bankrupt ourselves. This was the only way."

"And then what?" I asked. "What about when the population grows again? Are you going to attack them again?"

Ivan tilted his head up toward the stars, not answering.

"I know it's more than just about farmland. I'm not stupid. You want more power, too," I said.

"Of course," Ivan said. "Are you familiar with the kings of old, who united the Areth continent under one rule?"

I shook my head.

"The first to do it was Kudi the Great. His rule ushered in a golden age. There's even some evidence that with the crystal mages and his benevolent rule, they had technology that surpassed our current level of progress. It all declined in time once magic was purged from the world. If you get a chance to see some of the ruins in Panderica sometime... you can imagine what the world once looked like."

I'd never thought much about past ages. I presumed people were people, just like us, working for their countries, trying to make sure their families ate and were safe. What would I have done in a prior age? I couldn't say. "And you would like to be Ivan the Great?"

Ivan chuckled. "You can call me that, if you like."

I prodded him in the side with my fingers, causing him to laugh harder.

"I'm serious," I said. "You want to take over the world, don't you?"

Ivan shrugged. "I believe I could do a lot if I had more resources at my disposal. With everything I'm researching, a new golden age is possible."

"I think things are pretty good as they are."

Ivan frowned as if considering my words. "They can always be better. It's easy to rest on one's laurels. But that's not me. I don't think it's you, either."

"If you think I'm going to be an instrument of your world domination plans, you're sorely mistaken. I'm going to work to make sure you *don't* invade other nations."

Ivan smiled. "A challenge. You're idealistic, but when you see the plans I have, I hope you'll come to a different conclusion. After all, it only took a year to change your mind on the benefits of marriage, did it not?"

He had me there. "You could always try romancing a girl instead of talking to me as if I'm one of your generals."

Ivan feigned a look of offense. "Did I not greet you with rose petals and music when you returned?"

"That was nice," I admitted.

Our eyes met again. Ivan stopped walking. So did I.

Ivan leaned in toward me. I panicked, not sure what I should do. I couldn't even move. He'd maneuvered me into thinking about so many other things I'd forgotten about us in the present.

He kissed me.

The touch came gentle and soft, tactical just like his way of thinking. The sensation made my lips tingle. It was much more than the quick peck he'd given me before. My flight instinct kicked in, and I wanted to run, but I stayed where I was.

Despite my instincts, I found I didn't hate the kiss. In fact, the soft manner in which he'd approached me, and yet the way his confidence shone through as if he had no doubt I was his, was a pleasant sensation. I found my breath stilled as he pulled back.

"I shall endeavor to romance you better, as you say."

It drove me mad how Ivan took into consideration everything I said and listened to me. I wanted him to say no, to fight back at my demands.

Give me a reason to hate you! It wasn't fair. I couldn't like him. Not after all this. Not after the way Ethan had looked at me like I had stabbed him in the chest. I allowed myself to breathe.

Ivan quirked the corner of his lip upward into a half-smile. "We are at your quarters. I look forward to tomorrow."

What was tomorrow? I blinked. Time had passed so quickly I'd nearly forgotten.

Tomorrow, I would be getting married.

CHAPTER 31

I DIDN'T WANT to get out of bed. Like so many events as of late, this had seemed like a moment which would never truly come, a bad dream which I would wake up from at any moment, but here I was. I pinched my arm to make sure it was real.

A red circle appeared on my arm. It stung. There was no escaping.

The servants moved me into a room they'd set up as a staging area, with mobile mirrors, a chair with a mechanical crank that raised and lowered it, and a mannequin which held the most beautiful dress I'd ever seen.

It was white as a pearl, and several pearls adorned it in tasteful places. The fabric sparkled. I could hardly believe my eyes.

"It's beautiful, isn't it? The cost of it must have been extraordinary," one of the servants said. "More money than I'll see in my lifetime, that's for sure."

Guilt swelled in me. With all the problems going on in the world, with people starving so badly in the Wyranth Empire that they'd form a resistance, how could Ivan buy something so opulent for me?

But it was there. I wouldn't waste it, nor would I take it for granted. The dress was beautiful. I would be beautiful. I wished this were for an occasion that filled me with joy instead of an empty sinking feeling.

Betraying Ethan.

I shook my head. No. I wouldn't let my thoughts devolve. I had to appreciate what I had, use the situation that life gave me to my advantage. I should be thrilled. How many girls could say they lucked into becoming an empress?

Was this my luck—or rather my blood—controlling events? Was I being guided into this position by a fate that demanded me be here? How much did my genetics dictate what was going on in the world around me? The thought made me more uncomfortable than the wedding itself.

I let out a deep breath as the servants guided me to the chair. They began mucking with my hair, yanking it with brushes.

"Ow," I said.

"Have to get the tangles out," one servant said.

They kept at brushing my hair for a long while, before working with a heated rod to give my hair some extra curls. With those, they pinned my hair into position.

I watched in the mirror as I was transformed from an ordinary girl into someone elegant. My hair was up, each strand carefully placed to give me a regal look. It was stunning.

Then, the servants went to work on my makeup.

They applied powders and blushes, accented lines on my eyelashes and reddened my lips. I didn't get to put on a face very often, and it brought me comfort, stilling my thoughts of at least a time.

Soon, they finished with their work.

I stood, surveying myself in the mirror. The servants had transformed me. I could almost believe an empress stared back at me. My face looked like porcelain, my cheeks rosy. My hair was immaculate. I hesitated to turn my head for fear it would fall out.

They brought the dress up to me and had me step into it before lifting it over my undergarments.

Marina came into the room just as they tied the dress on me, forcing me to suck my stomach in as they tightened it. I wasn't fat by any means, but I still felt uncomfortable with how small they forced my waist.

Marina canted her head at the mirror. "My my, Zaira. You are quite the looker."

"They can make anyone look beautiful with this much work," I said.

"Nonsense. You were beautiful to start. Now you're incredible. I can only imagine what your groom will be thinking." She grinned mischievously.

"Stop it," I said, wrinkling my nose.

"Don't make faces. You'll smudge the makeup," the servant said.

"Sorry," I said.

They continued working on making sure the dress held in place as Marina came closer.

"Are you nervous?" Marina asked.

"Not really."

"You've been quite the talk of the Rislandian camp," Marina said.

"Oh?" I asked.

"Everyone was skeptical of your marriage at first, but they're already seeing the results in the way the Wyranth are acting. There's talk that there might even be a formal peace treaty between the Iron Emperor and Queen Reina as a result of the discussions here."

"At least I've been useful for something," I said. Even if it was just getting pieces of paper signed because of being used as a bargaining chip, I'd done something worthwhile. It's all I ever wanted to do.

"You're useful for a lot more, Baronette," Marina said. "I hope that when this all settles, you'll be allowed to come back and command an airship again."

"Me too," I said. Though I doubted Ivan would let his new valuable prize gallivant off as such. Especially on behalf of Rislandia. He'd been accommodating so far, but there had to be a line I couldn't cross.

The servants finished putting the white dress on me. I turned around to look at myself from different angles. No matter how I saw it, I looked perfect. Beautiful lace, an incredibly textured fabric on the dress. It fit my form perfectly. I was never one to have conceit about my looks, but I couldn't imagine someone being more beautiful than I was at that moment, even Queen Reina.

After I'd inspected myself and everyone admired the work, they rushed me out to another area of the residence, where gaslamps had been set in front of windows which overlooked the ocean beyond.

"A quick photo," a man in a suit said, standing behind a camera on a wooden tripod. I stood in front of the window, and he looked into the lens. A flashbulb went off, and I tried to hold a smile.

"Very good," the man said.

James came bounding in right after the picture had been taken. He made his way up to me like he owned the place, looking me up and down—first, in shock, and then second with a twinkle in his eye. "Wow, Zair-bear, I may have made the wrong choice in the princess."

"Shut up and stop looking at me like that," I said, shoving him away playfully.

James laughed. "You're beautiful, though. For real."

"Thanks," I said, feeling myself blush.

James glanced around and then lowered his voice. "Are you sure you want to go through with this? I can get you away in the mecha armor. We can make a run for it."

"We still need the information from Ivan about the airship," I said. "Only he knows how to make the crystals work, and where to find them."

"Crystals?" James asked, confused.

Right. He'd been away and hadn't heard the stories of the crystals, even when I'd returned to Rislandia to brief everyone the first time. "Never mind. What matters is, Ivan has the airship plans. Rislandia needs them."

A chill ran down my spine. Some wave of dread hit me, causing me to turn and look outside the window. A few birds flew in the distance, a little too far for me to make them out clearly, but they were small dark spots in the light of day. I wished I could fly away with them—or even that I could take James up on his offer. This was all so wrong, but the events had made things so much better for my people already. I had to stay strong and keep my commitments.

"You sure you're all right, Zair-bear?" James's voice became tender, in a way I'd only heard him a few times. It was when he was truly concerned about me.

"I have to be," I said, barely able to choke out the words. I had to compose myself. There was no way I could fall apart. I had to get through this.

"Are you ready?" one of the servants asked.

I nodded. "Let's go."

James and Marina accompanied me from the residence along with the servants, leading me to the outside of the building.

Kristina stood waiting for me. She'd been leaning on a pillar and pushed off of it when she saw me. "Excuse me. Might I have a moment with the bride?"

James narrowed his eyes. "Who are you?"

"It's okay, James. She's the Iron Emperor's sister." She probably had some last-minute plans to go over with me. With the battle outside, and Ivan having to track down resistance members and meet with Rislandians, there hadn't been time to go over a formal plan together, or to do a rehearsal. It was unusual, especially with a state wedding like this, but all of these circumstances have been unusual surrounding this day. Nothing in my life was ever normal.

The others moved on ahead, leaving Kristina and me to talk.

"You're about to be my brother's bride," Kristina said. "I may tease him, and have a little bit of a rivalry, but he is still my blood, you understand?"

She was so serious and poignant in the way she stared me down that all I could do was nod. Those same blue eyes as Ivan sank into me, icy cold and penetrating. I slouched nervously to one side.

"Good," Kristina said. "I know this is done under the guise of some nonsense about crystals, and he sees it as a political alliance with your kingdom which will transform the landscape of this peninsula, but there's more to it than that."

"There is?" I asked, my voice much higher than usual. How had Kristina transformed me into a helpless little girl with a mere stare?

"Of course there is. I've heard him talk about you. I've seen the way his eyes light up when he does. And I've seen the way he looks at you." She pointed a finger right at me, pressing it against my sternum. "He adores you. If you hurt him, I will slit your throat. Do you understand?"

My mouth went dry and my whole body numb. Ivan adored me? But this was all for his machinations. He'd never alluded to anything else, had he? I thought about the rose petals, the music, the way he'd opened up to me and kissed me the prior evening. Could it be he loved me?

I found it hard to believe he had the capacity for such feelings. He'd shown his human side to me, true, but nothing so strong nor forward. Other than the recent kiss.

I brought my fingers to my lips. It made me feel so small. Here I was worried because he might love me, as if this were a bad thing.

But how could I proceed with such knowledge? It made it all the much harder. Even though I'd grown to like Ivan, I wasn't sure I could ever love him, not like that. We were too different, and he had caused far too much pain to my people and me.

"Answer me," Kristina demanded.

"I'll try."

"You'll try?" She gave me a soft push with her finger, causing me to stumble before turning. "You'd better do more. You don't just hold the fate of two countries in your hands, you hold my brother's heart."

Kristina turned and paced away from me, each step with confidence, her head held high. She brushed against James, causing him to stumble as she passed.

"Hey!" James said, but he turned and jogged to come back to me. "Zair-bear, is everything okay? She seems *mad*."

I watched Kristina go on ahead and join a group of Wyranth down the path.

"Yeah, it's fine," I said, though, in truth, it was anything but fine. I was in too deep to turn back now.

James frowned and then nodded. "Let's go, then. We shouldn't be late."

"Yeah," I said, dragging my feet toward the grassy area down by the shore. My feet became heavy, like they'd been filled with lead. I wanted to scream.

No matter how much I wanted to run away, I was trapped.

CHAPTER 32

MY FRIENDS WALKED ahead of me while I shuffled slowly behind.

The scene would have been the most picturesque I could have imagined under any other circumstances. A small structure was built along the water to keep the wedding party out of the sun. A full symphony played along the beach, waves softly crashing against the shore through the music. Rose petals lined the lawn. Hundreds of people gathered in the seating area, wearing fancy dresses and dark suits. The women carried umbrellas, and the men wore top hats.

The only thing that marred the beauty of the moment was that half of these people were Wyranth, and at the structure, standing waiting for me along with a minister wearing all white, was Ivan, the Iron Emperor. He wore an elegant tuxedo with no hat, a black tie, and a red handkerchief protruding from his breast pocket. His blue eyes fell upon me and my dress, soft, caring. Could it be Kristina was right—Ivan *loved* me?

I tried to remember to breathe. I couldn't just stand here, but had to press ahead. I had to act with dignity.

I stepped to the carpet aisle. Candles stood on long brass stands, burning and smelling of cinnamon. Though it was light out, they added to the beautiful ambiance surrounding me. I stared off into the vast ocean beyond, a deep blue just like Ivan's eyes—vast and full of wonder. I swallowed and continued forward.

The symphony transitioned their song to a light-hearted and upbeat tune. I hadn't heard it before, but it was a fitting song for a future empress. But would I fit the role? It didn't matter. The decisions had been made for me.

Each step forward seemed to take an eternity. As I came closer to Ivan, I spotted the Rislandian delegation seated on the left-hand side. James and Marina hurried into seats by Talyen and Queen Reina. My father stood at the front, under the shade of the structure, watching with a somber countenance. He smiled when he saw me in my dress all the same.

I scanned the crowd. One person was absent—Ethan. My heart constricted.

But I couldn't stop moving, nor could I let my face show any distress. The wedding photographer had his head bent over under a sheet, looking through the leas of a camera off to the side, snapping photos of the crowd and me. Another reminder that this occasion would be recorded, remembered forever.

I pressed forward and moved up to the structure, stepping under it. Once out of the sun, my face cooled, and a soft breeze from the ocean gently blew over us. The air was salty but fresh.

Ivan smiled. "Welcome," he said.

The minister raised his hands upward. "The bride is here. Let the ceremony begin."

The Wyranth clapped heartily, but the Rislandian applause had trepidation to it.

The minister stepped forward, I stood on one side of him, Ivan on the other. The crowd watched the three of us, and the minister raised his hands.

"Friends and neighbors," he said. "We gather here today for a momentous occasion. A union, more than just two people, but truly, a union that represents the joining of two countries."

He paused to survey the crowd. "We all have our differences, and at times, it seems impossible for us to resolve them, but it goes to show that two people can make a difference. They can change the course of history."

He nodded toward Ivan. "The first emperor of our great Wyranth Empire was one such man. Shunning the ways of witchcraft from the north, he set off to create a better life for himself and his people, and so toiled in the more difficult lands of the south, but he prevailed. Through the efforts of Emperor Tyran The First, a new people grew, a people who have stood together for hundreds of years."

He turned to look at my father and beyond to Queen Reina. "It is my hope we can stand together now, not as Wyranth or Rislandians, but as people together, sharing in a joyous union between two of the most cherished members of our nations, Emperor Ivan the Fourth, and Baron Zaira von Monocle." He paused for applause.

"With their union, we hope to usher in a new era of peace and prosperity between our peoples. Let the relationship of this couple be a guide to all of us, on how to work together, how to love one another, and how to set our eyes upon the common goals for the betterment of all mankind." The minister turned to a table behind him. On it stood three candles. He lit two of them, handing one to Ivan and one to me.

The minister lowered his voice. "Set the candles toward the third on the table together, as a symbol of your unity."

I looked into Ivan's eyes, intense, deep, beautiful as they always were—and deadly serious. It filled me with nerves anew.

Butterflies fluttered in my stomach as I turned toward the table. I took my steps, the sweat on my palms making my skin feel clammy as I moved the candle forward.

Beyond the table was the sea. Waves crashed against the shore. The sky remained bright, with few clouds. A perfect, beautiful day. Only those birds flew in the background, breaking up the blueness of the sky and ocean. They seemed a long ways off. How could they fly for so long without coming ashore?

I set the thought out of my mind, moving in unison with Ivan to press our flames forward onto the third candle. A soft flame arose from it, flickering in the light wind.

The gathered crowd clapped again.

We kept the candles in our hands, returning to the minister.

"And now the vows," the minister said. "Emperor Ivan of Wyranth, do you hold sacred this woman before you, and promise to be true to her, to care for her, to love and cherish her, to hold her as your sole wife from now until eternity?"

"I do," Ivan said.

I held my breath. It would be my turn soon. Could I do it? These words... they meant so much. I had to be honest.

The minister opened his mouth to speak, but a little girl in the front row interrupted him.

"Mommy, those birds are coming toward us," the little girl said.

Her mother looked horrified at the interruption. "Dear, be quiet."

The crowd had already taken notice of the birds.

I'd been distracted by their flying twice, and now that I peered in the direction a third time, I recognized something unnatural about them. Their flight patterns didn't have the natural swoops of birds. The movements were much more rigid.

The crowd took notice as well, muttering swelling amongst their ranks. Ivan frowned.

The minister held his hands up. "Settle down, everyone. We can go see the birds when we're finished here. We—"

"No," Ivan said, his gaze falling toward the shore. He moved toward the table, setting the candle down and then stepping past it. He got up on the rocks along the edge of the land and placed his hand over his eyes to block the sun and get a better view.

I hurried over the best I could in my dress, hoping to get a good look along with him. "What do you see?" I asked.

"Those don't look like birds at all," Ivan said. "Bats?"

Bats? I narrowed my eyes. The creatures kept coming closer, and they grew in our view.

"Please, we should finish the ceremony," the minister said.

"You serve at my behest," Ivan snapped, not looking back. His words silenced the minister.

I kept my focus on the birds—bats—whatever they were. They had such familiarity to them. I'd seen the way they'd moved before.

It dawned on me exactly where I recalled their images from, like a camera's flashbulb going off in my head. The bats didn't move naturally, but mechanically. The wings flapped in a stilted manner, one which became clearer as they came into view.

My heart quickened, but my breath stilled. This couldn't be happening. Not here. Not now.

I stumbled backward, bumping into the table. My awkward movement caused the unity candle to fall over, catching the cloth on fire.

The minister panicked, blowing on the candle, and then using the cloth to set out the fire. "My word," he said.

"Zaira?" Ivan asked.

The candle didn't bother me, nor did the wedding any longer. "We're in a lot of danger. Get everyone out of here. We're not ready for this," I said.

"What is it?" Ivan asked.

The guests rose from their seats, several Rislandians moving forward to try to get closer to me, though Wyranth guards held them at bay.

"Zaira? Are you okay, my darling?" my father asked.

"Those aren't birds," I said. "That's an army. They're Nightmen." And there could only be one reason they were here.

CHAPTER 33

"NIGHTMEN? THE GIANT-BLOODED people you told me about from the Zenwey continent?" Ivan asked. "What could they want with us here?"

"I don't know, but wherever they went before, it was to enslave humans. We need to get everyone out of here," I said.

Ivan nodded. He summoned General Gregor, who joined us. "Get the guests to safety and ready the automatons for combat."

"Yes, sir," Gregor said. He made his way into the crowd, shouting orders to the Wyranth soldiers. The crowd seemed confused, but the majority of the Wyranth exited in an orderly fashion.

The Rislandians were another story.

My father and James had tried to get past the Wyranth guards and now engaged in a shoving match. My eyes went wide. This couldn't end well for my friends if it came to blows.

I brushed past Ivan and made my way to the soldiers. "Stop fighting!" I said.

The Wyranth stopped, glancing at me strangely, but they obeyed my orders.

"Let them through. That's my father and my best friend," I said.

"What's going on here, Zaira?" my father asked.

"The Nightmen. They're just off the coast. They'll make landfall any minute."

"This can't be good," my father said. "Our priority will be to get Queen Reina to safety."

"I can do that," James said. "Maybe I can help fend them off in my mecha armor."

"Not a bad idea," my father said. "We'll mobilize some of the soldiers to assist the Wyranth."

"Much appreciated," Ivan said.

My father shook his head. "Can't believe I'm about to work together with Wyranth, but I read your report, Zaira. I know exactly how dangerous these Nightmen are."

We should have been protected by a vast ocean. It must have strained their resources to get over here. But why now? It didn't matter. Shoot first, ask questions later. It was the von Monocle way.

"I need to get out of this dress," I said.

"I'll have my servants get you clothes."

I glanced back to the sea. The Nightmen's bat gliders were coming into better view. There wouldn't be much time before they would be swooping down over us, dropping their explosive bags. "Let's go," I said.

Ivan's servants led me back into the residence while the others went their separate ways. Rislandians grabbed all the arms they could find and joined the Wyranth for battle. It was an odd sight, the two clashing colors of uniforms standing side by side together, but this was the result I'd wanted, right? Peace between our peoples.

The cost could be greater than I imagined, and it wasn't just my happiness at stake now.

The servants helped me to get out of the dress and back into my normal clothes. Something was missing. "My cape," I said.

"It'll just make you a target," Ivan said.

I shook my head. "It's important. Trust me."

One of the servants found my cape and produced it, and helped get it around my neck. It flowed behind me in its crimson gloriousness. It brought me comfort.

I could move a little faster now. Ivan waited for me outside the room.

"We have to get you to safety," Ivan said.

"No way. I'm fighting to protect my people," I said.

"Zaira," he warned.

"I never led from behind when I was on the airship, and I'm not about to start now."

"At least get to a safe place with General Gregor. You know more about these Nightmen than anyone. Your information is more valuable than you would be as a grunt on the battlefield."

I crossed my arms, ready to argue, but he was right. I nodded. "Fine. Lead the way, but I'm not evacuating."

"I don't intend to, either. I have my empire to defend," Ivan said.

He led me through the dirt streets of the cove back to the fortified tower on the opposite side of the town. "We'll get the best view from here. Gregor will be able to manage the automatons, and we'll be out of the firing range of most of the line."

"Except their fliers are fast," I said.

"My sharpshooters will be faster," Ivan said.

I clutched at the hilt of the pistol holstered at my side. Having the weapon there meant the world to me. It was a little bit of safety in this strange land.

As we walked, several soldiers joined us, all Wyranth except one—Marina.

"Baronette," she said, adjusting the strap which held a rifle to her back.

"What are you doing here?"

"Guarding you by order of Queen Reina," Marina said.

When did I become so important to everyone? No, I knew the answer. The peace of two kingdoms depended on me. It made me uncomfortable, like I was more of a bargaining chip than a person. All I wanted was to be back on my airship.

Regardless of what I wanted, we moved back up the tower. Guards positioned themselves at the bottom, and Marina and two Wyranth joined us in the tower. Gregor was already there, along with Dr. Metzengerstein. The scientist had a strange control system he used for the automatons, while Gregor gave him orders. The controls had several levers and dials, along with strange antennae protruding from it. As much as I was curious as to how it worked, now wouldn't be the time to ask.

The Nightmen made landfall as soon as we made it up the tower. They engaged the automaton army, dropping explosive bags. The automatons could do little to resist, explosions sending their ranks flying, some into the sea, and others bursting into small pieces. Those bags were much more powerful than bullets, something Ivan hadn't accounted for in the design of these constructs.

"We have to spread them out," Gregor said.

"Easier said than done in that space," Dr. Metzengerstein said.

I clutched my pistol, even though I knew it wouldn't do much good at this range. Even the riflemen held their fire as the first wave of Nightmen gliders overwhelmed them.

There had to be dozens of ships—gliders and their transports. This was no small expedition they'd sent out. They had a frightening force, which, as it came closer, formed a dark cloud in the sky, casting a shadow down below.

The civilians ran, Wyranth evacuating them as best they could. They pushed through the town and out the gates on the other side while the automatons and military men dutifully fired on the Nightmen fliers.

Our people managed to shoot a couple of the gliders out of the air, but the explosive bags pelted the wedding grounds as I'd never seen before, clearing the whole area of our forces. Our men retreated, and the Nightmen transports set down.

Dozens of Nightmen came out of the ships, wearing dark armor and leathers, and brandishing rifles. Bullets flew back and forth. The battle was an intense scrum, impossible for me to get a read of what was going on.

General Gregor did his best, giving orders upon orders to a nervous Dr. Metzengerstein, who had sweat dripping down his face.

For every Nightman who fell, two others took his place. Their numbers were astounding.

Our soldiers and automatons backed into the town proper, and from there used the buildings as cover for the approaching Nightmen force.

I could see the enemy more clearly now. They had black helmets, with black armor over their chests, and dark leather clothing beyond that which covered the rest of their bodies, making them harder to spot in the shadows. Their bright white eyes with red pupils were poignant, though, even from these distances.

The riflemen opened fire down below. Marina joined the Wyranth, scoring a hit on a Nightman right away, while the others had missed. I couldn't help but swell with pride in my guard and friend.

The fliers cut through, two gliders coming our direction. The Nightmen spotted us up on our tower, firing guns and tossing explosive bags toward us. We all ducked, and the riflemen fired at the Nightmen.

Marina hit one of the bags with a bullet mid-air, which exploded far enough away from us not to damage the tower.

The riflemen managed to pick off the pilot of the closest glider, and the glider crashed into the stone bricks below us.

It shook us, several explosive bags detonating upon impact, though it didn't break the stone infrastructure of the tower. Flames rose briefly from the crash but died just as quickly.

The second glider nearby us went down shortly thereafter, but a safe distance away from the tower.

"Perhaps this isn't the safest place to make a headquarters," Ivan said.

Gregor frowned. "There's nowhere in Carnait Cove that isn't exposed. My advice would be for you and your bride to take a horseless carriage and return to the capital."

"Noted," Ivan said.

Gregor shook his head but returned to commanding the automaton movements.

I kept a grip on my pistol holster, wishing I was in the action. Our forces were overwhelmed. They needed every man they could get. I glanced at Ivan, wondering what was going through his head as he stared at the battle through his cool, blue eyes.

The Nightmen continued their push. Every time I blinked, they gained ground. The Rislandian and Wyranth soldiers fired their guns around the corners of buildings, but with the amount of Nightmen advancing, they wouldn't be able to continue the fight for long. Something had to give.

If only I had my airship...

The Nightmen made their push, bat gliders flying around the buildings, swooping too quickly for our soldiers to get a good aim on them. They dropped explosive bags, and our people rolled away from the blasts. The side of one of the buildings collapsed, trapping a man beneath it. I winced, but couldn't look away.

"I should be down there," I said.

"You'd just get killed," Ivan said.

I bit my lip, not liking to be in this position. I was used to having authority, even if others didn't want me to go into battle. Now, I was a subordinate. But our people needed an edge. The von Monocle luck—or the giant powers—whatever Ivan wanted to call it. My presence might be enough to turn the tides. "You have to trust me, Ivan. I can do some good. My heritage will keep me safe."

He turned to me, but as he did, the ground pounded in the courtyard beyond us. The stone walls of the tower shook, loosening pebbles and dirt which trickled from the top of the tower down its sides.

I glanced over the wall as the shaking continued.

The two mecha units bounded forward. Each footfall was like its own mini-earthquake. Our giants had arrived, and they were mechanical ones.

CHAPTER 34

ETHAN AND JAMES fired their mecha's projectiles simultaneously. Smoke billowed from the giant mechanical arms as the ammunition pounded forward—cylindrical, but with a point—the exploding shells we would have used in airship cannons. They connected with a mass of Nightmen infantry ahead, erupting into an explosion that sent the enemy soldiers flying.

The scene became morbid, rank with death from the shots. I couldn't count how many of the Nightmen fell, but it was a lot of them.

The two mecha units pressed forward, awkwardly moving each step in those giant frames that must have weighed an incredible amount. I wondered how many more projectiles could be loaded into those arms.

I didn't get to find out the answer just yet, as the boys raised their other arms to blast flames forward. The heat forced the enemy Nightmen back, and finally, they were on the retreat.

But the bat gliders swooped around again, this time circling the mecha for prey.

James and Ethan swatted at the gliders, but the movements of the Nightmen's flyers proved too quick and agile for them. The mecha, while powerful, did not move at high speeds. What they gained in strength, the knights in the mecha armor lacked in quickness.

I glanced at Ivan. He had the earth crystal in his hand, turning it repeatedly. I'd noticed the action several times before but hadn't inquired about it when I saw it. Now I realized it was a sort of nervous tic.

"Are you okay?" I asked.

"Those mecha units were a sizable investment for the Wyranth Empire. I don't relish seeing your Rislandian knights piloting them."

"It seems like they're doing a good job to me."

"Hmph," Ivan said, continuing his ritual of turning the crystal in his hand.

And they were doing a great job. They pushed the Nightmen back, allowing our soldiers to regroup and form better positions. James and Ethan used their armor as bludgeons, swinging their arms back and forth, mowing over Nightmen with each movement.

But as fast as they took the Nightmen down, more came. The Rislandian advance became a stalemate, and soon, Ethan and James couldn't keep the Nightmen back. The enemy realized how slow these mechas were, and moved around them, evading their reach and claiming more ground.

The two mecha still managed to disrupt the Nightmen ranks, plowing through the middle of them, slowing the advance, but the Nightmen and our soldiers renewed their battle, bullets flying back and forth.

After a time, Dr. Metzengerstein stepped back. "That's the last of our automatons," he said.

"Impossible," Ivan said.

Dr. Metzengerstein shrugged. "They've all been incapacitated."

"Regrettable. I wish I'd brought a larger force."

General Gregor frowned. "You couldn't have anticipated an attack of this scale," he said.

Yet more Nightmen fliers appeared in the sky. They would make landfall shortly. There were too many of them. Even with Ethan and James's near-invincible armor, there was only so much they could do.

The Nightmen cleared an area around the two mecha units, and fliers pushed toward them. They dropped explosive bags on the mecha units. One of them lost its footing and fell over. Whatever metal they were made of was strong enough to absorb the blasts—it retained all of its parts—but it couldn't keep upright.

"Ethan!" I found myself yelling, though he wouldn't be able to hear me.

Ivan cocked a brow at me but returned his attention to General Gregor and Dr. Metzengerstein. "It's a shame we couldn't have brought the crystal device. We could use it just about now, use the ground against the enemy."

"It will be some time before I'm able to create a portable unit," Dr. Metzengerstein said.

One of the large troop transport carriers landed near the base of our tower. The guards below engaged with them, but were soon overrun by Nightmen.

"They're coming!" I said.

"I can see that," Ivan said.

The riflemen beside us fired their guns downward, taking down a couple of the invaders, but more came—and they entered the stairwell where they couldn't be shot. Our men changed their positions, pointing toward the open stairwell. We had a better position, but how many of them had made it up the stairs? In the flurry, I couldn't be sure.

I pointed my gun down into the winding stairwell, though the others made sure Ivan, Gregor, and I were positioned such that we would not be the first targets upon Nightmen firing.

My heart pounded as we waited for the enemy. We might have had the high ground, but we were trapped with nowhere to go. If they outnumbered us...

The Nightmen came. Guttural shouting echoed through the stairwell, and then I could see their angry dark eyes upon us.

Guns *cracked* as both sides fired their weapons. Bullets zinged all too close to me, but I held the aim of my pistol steady.

One of the Wyranth soldiers took a bullet to the face, spinning and falling beside us. One less defender from the onslaught.

The Nightmen took casualties of their own. Enclosed and in a line up the stairs, they were easy to pick off. Three of them collapsed from our bullets, but with all of us firing, it was difficult to say who landed the killing blow.

A Nightman threw an explosive bag toward us. This was what worried me most of all. One well-placed bag and all of us could be blown to bits, and it wasn't as if we had anywhere to go to evade it.

With my gun at the ready, I shot the bag out of the air. It exploded in the stairwell, shaking our stone tower, the ceiling crumbling where it exploded. The blast was far enough away not to hurt any of us, but the interior of the stairwell began to crumble.

It collapsed on the Nightmen inside, debris falling on top of the lead soldiers making their way to us. The stone cracked and fell, sealing the way up to us on the tower. It would take someone crawling over rubble to be able to pass now, and no more Nightmen came after the debris had settled. We were no longer a viable target—but we were also trapped up here.

I turned my attention back to the larger battle. The Nightmen pushed outward again, despite Ethan and James doing everything they could to hold them back. The two knights retreated to a position past the main landing point where the Nightmen had regained control, trying to stop the hordes of soldiers from rushing forward toward our meager defenses.

Even though my friends fought valiantly, there was no way for them to withstand such a force. We'd lost. It would be a matter of minutes before all of Carnait Cove was overrun. Would we be taken as prisoners or be executed?

I shivered. So much for my von Monocle luck.

Dr. Metzengerstein frowned. "Is there a way to rappel down the side? Perhaps I could repair some of the automatons if I could get to them."

General Gregor glanced downward beyond the tower wall. "We don't have a rope that long. We'll have to wait it out."

"Unacceptable," Ivan said. "There has to be something we can do."

Marina pointed her gun over the wall and fired. She shot a Nightman dozens of yards away. I wouldn't have been able to aim so true at this distance. "We can take down as many as we can until they capture us."

My heart sank. After all we'd been through, all the planning, the sacrifices I'd made to ensure peace between the Wyranth and Rislandia, our work would be wiped away in moments by these strange invaders from a foreign continent.

How could the universe be so cruel?

Ivan fidgeted with his crystal in his hand. "I should have listened to you and fled when we had the chance," he said.

"Yes, you should have," Gregor said. There was no malice in his voice, but we couldn't change the situation we were in now.

Or could we?

"Ivan," I said.

"Hmm?" His blue eyes met mine. For the first time, I saw fear and despair in them. A face so used to confidence and winning, it was a shock to me that made my whole body tighten. He truly believed all was lost, and it shook my own confidence.

"The crystals. You said the mages of old used to command them with their will, right? That meant they didn't have any fancy machines to help them out. And you also said there was a synergy between male and female when using them, right? Why can't we try to use the crystal?"

"I've never been able to make it have any effects," Ivan said.

"By yourself."

Ivan frowned. "I don't suppose there would be any harm in trying, but I don't know the secrets to activate the crystal."

"Maybe it's just a matter of faith," I said.

Ivan held the crystal out to me, palm up. It was a brown piece of rock, and I would have never noticed anything special about it without Ivan telling me about its properties. He expected me to take it, but instead, I took his hand, entwining his fingers with mine, the crystal rock uncomfortably between our palms.

I guided our arms and pointed it outward, holding the crystal toward the scene of the battle ahead, the small protrusion of land where we'd almost gotten married, but now was tarnished by death.

I narrowed my eyes, focusing on the crystal, the Nightmen, and the ground ahead. This was the earth crystal, which meant I could command the dirt and rocks with it if I managed to figure out how to get it working, right?

Despite my intense focus, nothing happened. The Nightmen pushed further, driving the Rislandians back. Some of them overran our mechas, toppling Ethan and James to the ground, forcing them on their backs.

"It's not working," Ivan said.

"We can't let this happen," I said firmly. My friends and family were not going to die on my watch. Not like this, not now. Not after I'd toiled so hard to change this world. "Ivan, do you know the difference between now and the time it worked?"

"The machine that Dr. Metzengerstein created to make the power flow."

I shook my head. "No, it was more than that. You believed in the machine. You knew it would work. It's about your will."

"It can't possibly be that simple."

"It can. Trust me. Feel it."

Ivan's eyes narrowed as he focused.

Out in the battlefield ahead, the Nightmen overran our forces. One of the mecha units swung a leg out to stop their advance, but it was much too little, too late. If something was going to happen, it had to be soon.

The crystal warmed in my hand. At first, I thought it could have been because of the warmth of our two hands coming together, but then it became red hot. The heat caused my palm to sweat. The crystal vibrated in my hand.

"You believe. I can feel it," I said.

"You're crazy," Ivan said.

"You love it." I bit my lip, wishing I hadn't uttered those words. They hit too close to home. Still, I couldn't suppress a grin at the knowledge that his faith in me—his love for me—was making this happen. Honestly, I found myself caring for him too. It was something I'd have to sort out later.

The air thickened around our hands, and then around us as a whole. We were connected with this crystal. It flowed through us, and us through it. In some ways, it made me one with Ivan. I understood his hopes, his dreams, his fears... the sensation was so overwhelming it made me gasp.

"Focus," Ivan said.

I could have lost myself in him then, but there was the battle ahead of us—the Nightmen. We had to deal with them.

I held my hand up, along with Ivan's, our arms pointed toward the battle. Though I couldn't see anything, it was like a wave of air pushed forward, connecting with the dirt below us. Every particle was a part of me. It brought me strength, grounding. I pushed the energy forward with the help of Ivan. My cape rippled behind me.

The ground split where we focused our thoughts, creating a crack in the dirt road ahead of us, driving forward and opening as it reached the Nightmen. The ground shook, rattling even us back at the tower.

I stumbled.

"Don't worry. Keep your eyes on the goal," Ivan said.

The ground moved at our command. It rattled violently, causing the Nightmen to lose their footing. I focused, trying to make the earth crumble beneath them. Rocks and clumps of dirt flew everywhere. Another crack in the ground formed lengthwise, cutting off the wedding area from the rest of us. I directed the crack to form around the mecha units, keeping them on our side. A few Nightmen made it to our side, but our forces would be able to handle them.

The crack widened and deepened, making an impossible chasm from where the majority of the Nightmen forces had gathered. Hardly any remained on their feet as the ground shook so much, the very dirt below their feet collapsed.

The wedding area became an island, separated from the rest of the land. I watched as the chasm grew wider.

The Nightmen scrambled to their fliers, but it was too late. The ground gave way, and their landed vehicles collapsed along with them. The whole earth broke apart into tiny pieces, debris flying everywhere.

Then, the wedding grounds crumbled into the sea. The Nightmen struggled, but the drop was far too much for anyone to survive. Hands reached and tried to grab onto anything substantive, but nothing was there.

They sank and fell.

I'd killed them all.

The effort was too much for me. I couldn't believe the devastation I'd caused. The power flowing through me was far too much.

I met Ivan's eyes once more time. He looked at me in a new way, a manner I hadn't seen before. He was proud of me.

It brought me comfort, as I didn't want to think about all of the lives I'd taken.

Then, the force of all the power brought about an equal and opposite reaction, the wave of energy pushing back at Ivan and me. My knees buckled, and I collapsed.

The last thing I remembered was Ivan holding me in his arms, urging me to keep fighting.

EPILOGUE

I AWOKE IN Carnait Cove's inn. The bed I'd been sleeping in was still intact after all of the battles. I'd slept so long my head had a fuzziness to it, my eyes opening to see double. Someone had dressed me in a nightgown, and I'd been lying around so long my muscles were stiff.

What had happened? Last I recalled, I'd been able to use Ivan's earth crystal to cause a portion of the land to sink into the sea. It seemed like a dream. How could I have caused such destruction?

My whole life changed the first time I'd felt an earthquake in Plainsroad Village, and now I was able to cause them myself, at least with Ivan's help. Together, we'd become an unbelievable destructive force.

One I hoped I could influence Ivan to use for good.

I still didn't know the final outcome of the battle. The room was empty, with no one to greet me. A quiet stillness lingered in the air.

I supposed it could have been possible the Nightmen took over and left me here. Then, I would be a prisoner.

I swung my legs over the side of the bed, pushing myself to stand. My knees shook from weakness. I had to brace myself on the side of the bed.

After a while, I gained my balance. Each step forward had to be taken with caution, much more slowly than I liked to move. As I made it to the door of the room, my head finally adjusted and settled into normalcy, my haziness dissipating.

It occurred to me I probably should dress before heading out the door. No one wanted to see me in my nightgown. I turned to the closet where I found my typical garb of a white blouse and gold skirt, though I couldn't find the red cape that gave me my signature look. What could have happened to it after the battle? The answer would have to wait.

After dressing, I made it out of the room, down the hallway and to the stairs leading to the common area.

To my surprise, I found Ivan, my father, Queen Reina, General Gregor, and James, all gathered together, seated on different chairs and talking.

My father was the first to spot me. He stood. "Zaira! You're awake. Thank Malaky."

The others turned to stare at me.

I cautiously stepped down the stairs, and my father moved to help me by taking my hand and holding me steady the rest of the way. "How long was I asleep?" I asked.

"Three days," my father said.

"We won the battle," James said, as if reading my face and determining my first question. "I thought we were licked pretty good, but the ground opened up and swallowed the Nightmen whole. Crazy. They'll be writing songs about it, I'm sure."

My father guided me to a chair, and Ivan had one of the innkeepers bring me a cup of hot tea. The others greeted me and told me how nervous they'd been about my state while the tea brewed.

A server set a platter before me with cream and sugar. I poured myself a cup. The scent was a delightful blend of spicy cinnamon and a smooth floral, and I took a sip of the warm liquid. It took that moment to realize how parched I'd become. This was the first drink I'd had in days. I sighed, content.

"Matters have changed significantly since you went into your coma," Ivan said. "The crystal created an energy feedback which proved too much for your psyche. I have Dr. Metzengerstein working on a solution for it to protect us in the future."

I didn't much care about the crystals at the moment, though of course, it would be the first thing on Ivan's mind. "So the Nightmen are gone?"

"Yes and no," Queen Reina said, setting her teacup down.

"We were successful in the battle," my father said. "Their forces numbered five hundred in all. Your actions managed to take one hundred and fifty of them from the battlefield."

I couldn't help but shiver. I'd killed a hundred and fifty people in one wave of my arm? The thought harrowed me. Such a destructive power! Even though our airship held such deadliness when firing exploding shells, this seemed so much more personal.

"However," Ivan said, "we're also told this was merely a scouting expedition, the first foray of a much larger Nightmen invasion. The prisoners were rather smug, and told us it would only be a matter of time before we would all be enslaved."

I bit my lip, vividly remembering how the Nightmen took humans for slaves, and how they treated our kind. "They'll ravage our whole peninsula," I said.

"If we don't stop them first," my father said.

"Ivan, you have to give us the airship plans. We need to get the *Liliana* off the ground. Please," I said, eyes searching him, pleading. He had to understand that, wedding or not, we had to protect both of our countries.

His eyes met mine, serious and deep as ever. "No, not at this time," Ivan said.

"What?" I asked. My heart sank. I needed to be back on the airship. I was the one who had the power to put a stop to these

Nightmen, but I needed my crew and our arsenal. He couldn't possibly still want to hold this over us.

"I showed you some of our plans, but not all of them," Ivan said. "I'm sure you're confused and believe you would like to get back to your airship and Rislandia, but we have formulated a better plan together."

"Hear him out," Queen Reina said.

"On the Isle du Mystere, our engineers have been developing a Wyranth aerial fleet, one with a metal frame instead of a wooden one. It will be more robust, its speeds will be greater, and it will have a significantly more powerful arsenal than the Rislandian design. It also has the ability to carry smaller fighter craft and launch them. We'll be in need of those to counter the assaults of the Nightmen bat gliders."

This was news to me. I could hardly believe it. "Why not use both?"

"We may," Ivan said. "It will be a matter of how many of the air crystals we'll need to extract for the engine components. Queen Reina and I have come to an agreement to give my engineers access to your Crystal Spire, where I believe the air crystals have been buried."

So that's where they were hidden. It made so much sense. The crystals were why only Rislandia could build airships, and why the technology became lost so easily. "I want to fly again," I said, my voice coming out much weaker than I would have preferred. It was my only desire. I couldn't be trapped in some palace like a normal noblewoman. I was certain Ivan would think I was too important to do otherwise, but it wasn't fair.

"We aim to make that happen," my father said.

Ivan nodded. "It was one of the concessions I had to make for access to the crystals. Our new vessel will have a joint Rislandian and Wyranth crew. Though I believe you would be more valuable working directly with Dr. Metzengerstein and me, one of the conditions of our agreement will be that you will be the one to captain the aerial carrier."

For the first time in ages, my spirits lifted. All my sense of dread vanished. My father grinned at me. This was great news—at least, as great of news as I could figure while we were on the precipice of an invasion by some of the vilest creatures I'd ever come across. I'd be able to fly again. I'd be with my crew again. There was no way we could lose.

Did this mean I could still be a Rislandian? Did I have to marry Ivan? With the Nightmen looming over our continent, those questions seemed unimportant. I understood the danger, and so did everyone in the room. It was on me to do something about it.

I couldn't help but smile, despite all of my personal worries. "I accept the position. When do we take off?"

ALSO BY JON DEL ARROZ

The Adventures Of Baron Von Monocle:
For Steam And Country
The Blood Of Giants
The Fight For Rislandia
The Iron Wedding
The Steam Knight

The Saga Of The Nano Templar:
Justified
Sanctified
Glorified

The Aryshan War:
The Stars Entwined

Short Story Collection:
Make Science Fiction Fun Again

ABOUT THE AUTHOR

Jon Del Arroz is a #1 Amazon Bestselling author, "the leading Hispanic voice in science fiction" according to PJMedia.com, and winner of the 2018 CLFA Book Of The Year Award. As a contributor to *The Federalist*, he is also recognized as a popular journalist and cultural commentator. Del Arroz writes science fiction, steampunk, and comic books, and can be found most weekends in section 127 of the Oakland Coliseum cheering on the A's.

Twitter: @jondelarroz
Instagram: @jdelarroz
Website: delarroz.com
Email: jdaguestposts@gmail.com

www.ingramcontent.com/pod-product-compliance
Lightning Source LLC
Chambersburg PA
CBHW022143240626
47153CB00007B/2489